M'aidez

FOR RICHARD
WITH BEST WISHES
George A. Reynolds

M'aidez

George A. Reynolds

Pentland Press, Inc.
England • USA • Scotland

PUBLISHED BY PENTLAND PRESS, INC.
5122 Bur Oak Circle, Raleigh, North Carolina 27612
United States of America
919-782-0281

ISBN 1-57197-196-3
Library of Congress Catalog Card Number 99-74761

Printed in the United States of America

For Louie, Sarah, and all the guys and gals behind the yokes and mikes who have worked so hard to keep 'em flying.

For their kind, technical, and invaluable assistance in the writing of this story, a special thanks and my sincere appreciation to LTC Joseph L. Shannon, USAFR; LTC James W. Harrison, USAFR; Mr. Robert E. McIntyre; Mr. Gerald W. Hogan, EE, Karen Lake, Jami Potter, Lisa Blair, and Anita Lake of Birmingham, AL; Mr. George E. Strand of Honolulu, HI; Mr. H. S. Gann and McDonnell Douglas Aircraft Company in Long Beach, CA; the U.S. Army Aviation Museum in Ft. Rucker, AL; and the USAF Museum in Dayton, OH.

Chapter One

March 24, 1950—Day One

Bruce Ryan checked his luggage at the American-Mexican Airways ticket counter shortly after sunrise. Nagging feelings of dismay came over him as he ambled through the cavernous terminal building at Houston's Hobby Airport. He stopped by one of the floor-to-ceiling plate glass windows to look out across a broad asphalt ramp. No familiar Am-Mex DC-4s were parked there and he turned back to a row of seats nearby to continue observing the ramp. The small blue valise he had been carrying plunked to the terrazzo floor as he sat down slowly.

Bruce couldn't dispose of nor understand the dread that kept pulsing through him. He hadn't been afraid of flying since that first airplane ride five years ago. Momentarily, he glanced up and saw his father approaching from the automobile parking deck, coming along the same aisle Bruce had come down shortly before. Richard Ryan and Bruce looked almost like brothers. They were both six feet tall, 190 pounds with ash blonde hair, a ruddy complexion, and green eyes. But Richard's additional twenty-one years were beginning to show in shallow lines about his face.

"Did you find a close parking place?" Bruce asked as Richard sat down next to him.

"Yeah, there's not many cars in the deck yet," he replied.

There was a long silence as both men looked about the huge passenger area. After a few minutes Richard said, "Son, is there something wrong? Maybe you're upset about your mom not coming to see you off?"

Bruce laughed softly, "Nah, I knew last night she wouldn't come out here with us. She just doesn't like saying goodbye to anyone."

Richard grinned, "Well, you're still a little boy to her."

"Yeah, I know, and I'm only pushing twenty-four," Bruce joked.

"Well, that's just mothers, but we both hate to see you go that far away. How long is it for, three years?" Richard said.

"Yeah, but you know, I've controlled air traffic here for the CAA (Civil Aeronautics Administration, predecessor of the Federal Aviation Administration) almost five years, and other than some little trips in the Air Corps back in '45, I've never been out of Texas much. By signing up for Honolulu, the agency promoted me and threw in a pay raise too. I just want to see a little more of this old world while I have the opportunity. Tell mom not to worry about her baby boy."

Richard grinned. "Okay. Just let us hear from you regularly."

Bruce smiled and nodded, then looked out the window at a tug pulling a DC-4 Skymaster onto the ramp. It was gleaming silver with script letters above the passenger windows that spelled out American-Mexican Airways then trailed into a rainbow of colors covering the entire vertical stabilizer. "Well, it looks like they're bringing my bird out. It won't be much longer. I'll be glad to get started," Bruce said and a pang of dread hit him again.

"Yeah, you have quite a haul ahead of you. How long will it take to get there?" Richard asked.

"It'll be about four hours to Hermosillo. We'll be in Mexico an hour or so for a crew change and refueling. I think they told me it was a little over eleven hours inflight to Honolulu if the winds aren't too strong," he replied.

After a short wait the boarding call for Bruce's flight came. He shook hands with Richard and left with the other passengers. Twenty minutes later the plane leveled off at its assigned altitude. The air was smooth and a few puffy, yellow clouds floated by below as the engines began a steady cruising drone. Then two Mexican stewardesses started down the aisle dispensing soft drinks and snacks. Bruce glanced at the smoking sign above the cockpit door in front and lit a cigarette.

A man's voice with a Texan drawl began over the intercom system. "Ladies and gentlemen, this is Captain Holcomb, welcome aboard Am-Mex flight 501. We're cruising at six thousand feet and traveling at 230 miles an hour. Our arrival in Hermosillo will be

2

about 11:30 Pacific Standard Time. Two years ago today, 24 March 1948, American-Mexican Airways made its inaugural flight from Houston to Honolulu. So, we thank you for flying with us to begin our third year of operations."

He continued, "Just a little of our history for those who aren't familiar with the airline. We fly three days a week each direction. Our cargo is primarily medicine and tools for the mining section of northern Mexico along with thirty to forty passengers. Then from Mexico to Hawaii, we carry fewer passengers and our cargo is silver and copper ingots, leather goods, pottery, photographic supplies, vanilla extract, and tequila. The return flights bring musical instruments, flowers—especially orchids—ferns and of course, pineapple. Now for our Mexican national friends, our own flower, Maria, will repeat what I've said in her best Spanish. *Gozar el huida*, I think," he said as the Mexicans chuckled. The attractive girl smiled, repeated his message and said, "Enjoy the flight," in English. Her countrymen chuckled again.

Bruce decided he had time for a short nap. Almost immediately it seemed, a stewardess made the landing announcement to fasten seat belts and extinguish smoking materials. Waking up, he thought in jest, My belt is fastened, I'm not smoking, so land it.

At the airport terminal, ground crews scrambled about the aircraft removing baggage and cargo, started refueling procedures, and shortly began loading items destined for Hawaii. Then Bruce thought of his handbag, looked under the seat, and was relieved he hadn't forgotten it. He took out the bag, called an "AWOL bag" by the military and unzipped it. Yep, two cartons of cigarettes are here, my lighter fluid can isn't leaking, shaving kit, instant coffee, everything is intact, he thought and rezipped it.

Five crew members dressed in light blue uniforms came aboard and both stewardesses went to the galley at the plane's tail section. The three men went to the cockpit door and turned around. An average sized man with blonde hair and blue eyes said, "Ladies and gentlemen, I'm Charles Dane, your captain for the flight."

A smaller, slim man with dark hair and eyes said, "I'm Howard Pool, the alternate pilot/engineer."

The third man was larger and taller with green eyes and brown hair. He said, "I'm Harold McMorris, first officer. Glad to have you with us," and threw up his hand in a wave. They went into the cockpit and closed the door. The passengers turned their attention to other activities.

Bruce glanced out the window and saw a pickup truck filled with red, odd-shaped modules come up to the aircraft. A man got out and came aboard to talk with a blonde stewardess. She nodded; he left and waited by the truck until seven boarding passengers started up the stairway.

A dark-haired stewardess came forward with the passengers and began assigning them to seats, then checked off names on a manifest. Four of the Mexicans were obviously married couples and she seated them together. Two men appeared to be business acquaintances and sat together. The other man joined one of the Houston passengers, and a man who also boarded there sat alone.

The stewardess came to Bruce. "Mr. Ryan?" she asked.

"Yes."

"Sir, would you mind moving up and sitting with Mr. Myrick two rows forward? There are four no-shows for the flight, leaving only ten passengers and we want to bring cargo modules inside to occupy some of the empty seats. They contain delicate jewelry items that are easily broken."

"No, not at all. In fact, I've been a little lonesome sitting by myself," he responded.

She smiled. "Thank you very much, sir."

Bruce noted that she strongly resembled actress Gail Russell and had distinct, graceful curves in all of the right places. Dang! Those blue eyes light my fuse! Then, there's the short, raven hair and fair skin. Bet she's fully married too. Wish I'd checked for rings, he mused while getting his handbag. He went to the empty aisle seat, sat down, and turned to his companion while slipping the bag back under the seat.

"I'm Bruce Ryan. Looks like we'll be going to Hawaii together," he said, extending a hand and his eyes meeting the hazel eyes of his neighbor.

"Curtis Myrick. Welcome aboard my chariot," he responded, smiled, and shook his hand.

Bruce saw they were about the same size and guessed he was around thirty, but his thinning, light brown hair and freckled skin made it difficult to tell his age. "Are you from Houston?" Curtis asked.

"Yeah, a real native. Lived in the area all of my life. How about you, where are you from?"

"Oklahoma originally, but I've been in Honolulu since the war. I was there when it ended, and decided to take my discharge and stay. It seemed like a good deal then and it's worked out for me. I was an aircraft mechanic in the Navy and a local company offered me a job. What do you do?"

"I'm an air traffic controller with the CAA en route to Honolulu to work in the tower," Bruce replied.

"'Well, great! I think you'll like it there once you get settled and used to the system. Are you married?" Curtis asked.

Bruce smiled. "I'm twenty-three, but my mom thinks that's still too young. How about you?"

Curtis laughed, "Yeah, that's just like mamas. No, not anymore. I tried it during the war, when I was twenty, but within two years we both felt it was a mistake and parted company. Now at twenty-nine, I'm a confirmed bachelor for sure."

As they continued with small talk, Bruce noted that the ground crewmen had erected a temporary partition two rows back on both sides of the cabin. Then crewmen began stacking the odd-shaped modules into the seats, and from their actions in handling them they appeared to be heavy. Two small pegs on the inverted L-shape braces snapped into grooves in the air deck, then the packs were secured with belts, one in each seat. They finished and closed the door as an engine coughed, spun its propeller to life and started the plane trembling.

Both stewardesses came to stand at the closed cockpit door, and the dark-haired one picked up a microphone. "Ladies and gentlemen, I'm Janice Adams and this is Debra Huber. Welcome aboard Am-Mex flight 755. We'll be serving you for our flight to Hawaii." She continued with her message of safety, operating procedures aboard the aircraft, and emergency evacuation.

Bruce thought, Gail Russell's real name is Janice Adams. She is about five feet six, 120, and looks good enough to be a movie queen. Debra was shorter, put together nicely, had brown eyes, olive skin and a boyish blonde hairdo. Then Janice handed her the mike. She repeated the same message to the passengers in Spanish. As she spoke, Bruce was again aware of those pulsing jabs of dread he experienced before leaving Houston.

Chapter Two

The DC-4 taxied down the runway, hesitated, and started forward as its four engines revved simultaneously. Bruce could feel his body press back against the seat and glanced outside as the terrain began zipping by more rapidly with the passing seconds. Then he felt ground action stop and knew the landing gear had cleared the asphalt. Hmmm, the pilot used nearly all of the available 7,500 feet of runway, he thought as the end cropped up. We must be loaded extra heavily, or maybe the air is just thin here. It's not very hot outside.

"This is Captain Dane, ladies and gentlemen. Am-Mex flight 755 is now airborne. Welcome aboard. We're glad to have you with us for the ride to Hawaii. For obstruction clearance, we'll have to circle the airport until we reach an altitude of 10,000 feet, and then turn on course. After crossing the coastline, we'll descend down to 6,000 feet and you will be more comfortable. Please observe the smoking and seat belt signs above the cockpit door. You'll notice the smoking sign is off, so light up if you like, but leave your belt fastened until after the aircraft passes over the mountains. It gets pretty rough there sometimes, but we'll pass them shortly and you will be able to move about the cabin as necessary. You've already met our nice stewardesses and they will be serving you soon. Again, thank you for flying with Am-Mex and enjoy the flight." A second voice repeated the message in Spanish.

Bruce began fumbling for his cigarettes and noticed that Janice and Debra were buckled in the seats just behind him. He offered Curtis a cigarette. "No, thanks. I stopped those about the same time my wife and I called it quits," he said and grinned.

The aircraft continued climbing for fifteen minutes, then turned on course as the engines began receding to a steady, drumming tone. Now, rugged mountain ridges began slipping past 2,000 feet below and the plane seemingly bounced, dropped, and rocked, but groaning engines pulled it upward again. Some of the passengers held a hand over their stomach and laughed. Then the murky water of the Gulf of California came into view and, in the distance, the Baja Peninsula's mountains jutted upward beyond.

After a few moments, "This is Captain Dane, ladies and gentlemen. We've cleared the coastline and are now over the ocean. For those who wish to you may set your watch at 2 P.M. Pacific Standard Time. There will be two more time zones between here and Hawaii, and the stewardesses will be happy to advise you of the correct time as we progress. You may move about the cabin now as you wish. Thank you." That same voice repeated the message in Spanish as before.

Bruce noticed he had failed to reset his watch from Central Standard Time and did so as the aircraft began slowly descending to 6,000 feet. When they leveled off, Janice and Debra moved to the front of the cabin and began taking refreshment orders from the passengers. Bruce ordered coffee, Curtis decided on Scotch and water and paid the half dollar surcharge. Shortly they were drinking and making small talk as the flight continued.

Four hours later the stewardesses began serving meals and the aircraft started to bounce frequently in light turbulence. After their trays were cleared away, some of the passengers became uncomfortable as the roughness increased. "Ladies and gentlemen, this is Captain Dane. We're experiencing moderate turbulence as you know. Please return to your seats and buckle the belts. Traffic control will clear us for an altitude change shortly, so please bear with us a little longer, thank you."

Fifteen minutes later Bruce noted a change in the engine's tone and felt the aircraft climbing slowly. After ten minutes the turbulence decreased and the engines droned a steady beat. He assumed they were now at 8,000 feet based on the altitude rule for westerly flight. But he noted they were still experiencing slight jolts rippling through the fuselage. Shortly, he glanced out the window and saw the inboard engine's cowl flaps were open and sporadic puffs of blue smoke popped from the engine. Now, he could see a red glow inside the cowling and that the propeller was obviously turning slower.

Two hours more and the turbulence returned stronger than before.

"Ladies and gentlemen, this is Captain Dane. We're experiencing a small problem with an engine and can't climb immediately to get out of the turbulence again. Traffic control will clear us for a slower climb shortly. Bear with us, please. The stewardesses will do everything possible to make you more comfortable. Thank you."

After an hour, the right inboard engine's propeller spun to a halt with its blades feathered into the slipstream to reduce drag. "This is Howard Pool, ladies and gentlemen. We had to shut down one engine because of a problem with it. There is no cause for alarm. We'll be able to reach Hawaii fine. It will just take a little longer, however. We're unable to climb out of the turbulence zone right now, so please continue to bear with us on the roughness. We're very sorry. The stewardesses will continue to assist you in every way possible. Thank you, and we'll keep you advised as necessary."

Another hour dragged by and a series of jolts and bumps rippled through the aircraft that overrode the bounces and dips of turbulence. Bruce looked to the right first, then out the opposite window. Blue smoke was billowing from the outboard engine and shortly its propeller spun to a halt with its blades feathered. "This is Captain Dane, ladies and gentlemen. I'm sure you have seen that we had to shutdown another engine. Sometimes these things happen, and we regret the longer flight time and your concern. We're well past the halfway point between Mexico and Hawaii, and there is no real danger. The plane flies well on two engines. Traffic control has been advised of the situation. They are going to assist us in every way possible to expedite our arrival in Honolulu. Please bear with us. Our ladies will continue to assist you as needed. Thank you."

One hour later turbulence increased so that objects were being thrown about the cabin. "Ladies and gentlemen, this is Captain Dane. Regrettably, we can no longer maintain flying speed on two engines due to severe turbulence, a strong crosswind that was unforecast, and our gross weight. Also, our remaining engines are beginning to overheat. We have made a decision to ditch the aircraft while we still have power available and it's daylight. There is a much better chance of surviving our going into the sea this way. The stewardesses will go through evacuation procedures again for you, and traffic control has already alerted search and rescue about our situation. Remain calm, follow the instructions you are given, and we'll get out of the aircraft alive and injury free. We're sorry, and good luck to each of you."

Apprehension was rampant in the cabin as Janice began her message on evacuating the plane and Debra gave out bright yellow life vests. As she continued, the ten passengers became calm and listened to her instructions. "Pull your seat belts as tight as possible. Place the pillow on your knees, and when I yell, drop your face onto the pillow and place your hands on the back of your head. Remain in this position until the aircraft stops. Then move quickly but *do not run* to the emergency exits over the wing area. Flotation gear will be inflated at that time. Remember, *stay calm*. That is *very* important for everyone to get out safely. Remove your shoes now, and do *not* take any of your hand luggage with you. Good luck!"

Bruce now knew this was the dread he had had on his mind earlier.

Debra came forward and repeated her message in Spanish. Bruce had expected one or both of the women to show signs of the fear that gripped him but neither faltered in their speech or actions. The cockpit door swung open. Howard Pool took out four bundled, yellow rafts and placed them at the emergency exits. The aircraft continued to pitch and bounce, but leveled out as the engine changed to a tone of labored strain. Bruce looked down about fifty feet to the white capping waves that he guessed were at least six feet tall. Then he saw Dane and McMorris struggling to turn the plane's nose into the wind so the fuselage would hit the water parallel to the wave lines.

Before the aircraft touched down, Pool began assigning passengers to the life rafts. He told one of the married couples and a male passenger to join him in one. The other couple and a man were to follow McMorris into his raft. Debra and two men would be in a vessel with Dane. Bruce, Curtis, and Janice were to be in the other. This way, each raft would have a crew member included. Then Howard went to one of the rear seats and buckled himself in.

Bruce glanced around wondering whether all those modules would crash forward when the airliner hit the water. Debra was seated behind him and managed a quick smile when their eyes met for a moment. Janice and Howard were seated across the aisle behind him and both were staring intently at the open cockpit door. Dane's right hand came off the yoke and fell toward the air deck.

"This is it!" he called and placed his hand back on the controls.

"Now! Put your heads down now!" Janice yelled loudly, and Debra immediately repeated her words in Spanish.

Chapter Three

The Skymaster's first contact with the water sent tremors of shock through the fuselage as the tail hit. Then the engines flared and died. A crunching rumble echoed in the cabin as its nose settled into the waves, and passengers responded with various verbal retorts. When forward motion stopped, Howard rushed up and ripped open the emergency exit on the right side, then turned to the left and hesitated. "There's more water that way, folks. Let's all go out the right exit. Move steadily but don't push," he said as he stepped out of the opening to inflate the first raft on the leeward side.

People were moving slowly out when McMorris came from the cockpit and picked up a raft. Dane was right behind him, got two, and brought them to the exit. The aircraft began floundering slowly in the rough sea but showed no signs of sinking yet. All of the men and women stood on the wing while the rafts were being inflated from bottles of compressed air.

Steadily the DC-4's wing became awash, but soon all four rafts were inflated and the survivors got aboard. Winds blew misty spray over the men and women while they struggled to move their bobbing vessels away from the tottering plane. Captain Dane shouted to be heard above the wind noise. "Everyone, let's continue our efforts to clear the aircraft, then we'll tie the rafts together so they won't become scattered." In ten minutes, the rafts were bunched together and crew members were toiling to lash one to the other. Then a woman's voice soared above the din, "The plane is sinking. Thank goodness we all got out safely."

Finally, the rafts were secured and Dane polled the survivors. There were no serious injuries but a few reported bumps and bruises. Crew members advised their passengers about riding the craft, and each was told to remain seated as much as possible.

When twilight became more pronounced, dark clouds appeared in the northwest and seemingly stood just above the wave tops. The rafts were heading toward them slowly.

Engine noise rumbled above the shrieking wind as a DC-6 was suddenly overhead. It circled the area slowly and deliberately, then turned on its wing lights. Dane took out a signal mirror and waited until the plane approached him. Then he waggled the mirror until there was a bright glow. The plane's lights blinked three times and the aircraft began a lazy circle to pinpoint their location before it turned away eastward.

As the aircraft climbed upward waving its wings, Dane again shouted to the group. "Okay, everyone, they have our position and will relay it to search and rescue. Let's all try and relax until a ship or plane comes for us. I don't think it will be very long."

Howard Pool repeated Dane's message in Spanish and added, "The rafts have provisions and survival gear, so we'll be fairly comfortable except for being wet. Just sit quietly and wait it out. The crew will do everything we can for your comfort and welfare, but our main concern now is safety. Take it easy and don't make any sudden movements, you might fall overboard. Only move about slowly and no more than necessary for comfort."

Lightning flashed vividly in the northwest, and seemingly the small craft moved more rapidly toward the storm with passing minutes. McMorris began speaking. "Ladies and gentlemen, weather service told us before our flight that a frontal system was coming down from north of Hawaii, but it wasn't supposed to arrive there until late tonight. Apparently, it moved faster than expected. Those are thunderstorms we're seeing now, and that's the reason for the strong winds we encountered before. When this storm gets to us we'll have very gusty conditions and heavy rain. Sit still and hold onto the lines that are around the top edge of your raft. They won't sink, but it's going to be rough," he said as thunder rumbled closer to them.

Complete darkness fell as the heavy, wind-swept rain plummeted over the small band of survivors. The rafts began bobbing and tugging at the restraining lines that lashed them together. Thunder cracked and lightning flashed constantly as the rain's intensity increased. The survivors clung to lines on the vessels and looked at fellow travelers on the other rafts with heavy skepticism in the winking light. An occasional verbal retort came from the group amid claps of thunder, and although he didn't speak Spanish, Bruce recognized the words of the Lord's Prayer being recited by one of the Mexican ladies.

Wind, rain, and large waves continued to lash at the undulating raft with a vengeance. Bruce had difficulty holding the valise he had smuggled aboard. Janice was sitting in the bow of their vessel and jerked with fright when the line securing it to the others snapped back over her. She called to the crew members, but only Curtis and Bruce heard her above the howling wind. As the black wetness continued, Curtis told his companions their raft was rapidly becoming waterlogged and unless each began bailing immediately, they would be in danger. All three of them cupped their hands and started dipping out water.

From the back of the raft Bruce could see Janice and Curtis only when lightning flashed, but he noted they were bailing as steadily as he was. Tinges of nausea stabbed at him and he dropped his head to his legs. Rising after a moment, he saw Curtis in the middle section continuing to bail and guilt rippled through his mind. He swallowed several times and resumed bailing. Suddenly, the rain stopped and a wind shift was apparent. The raft oscillated momentarily before it swung around and started running steadily with the wind. Light rain began as lightning continued to flash and move steadily ahead of them.

Janice called out, "Are both of you okay?"

"Yeah, how about you?" they replied simultaneously.

"So far so good, but the other rafts broke away from us. Maybe we'll be able to see them again after daylight," she said.

The three occupants continued to bail water from their raft, and now that the rain had diminished, they were able to tell progress had been made and the danger had lessened.

Day Two

Light was very long in coming to the chilled survivors, but at last a little brightness appeared while the wind shrieked and misty rain fell intermittently. Sunlight increased slowly and the rain finally ended. Bruce checked his watch and noted it had been twelve hours since the aircraft went down. The watch showed Pacific Standard Time and he knew it was about two hours ahead of the local time, but he wasn't sure what zone they were in and left it as it was.

All three of them began looking for signs of the other rafts. However, there was nothing in sight except ocean and a high cloud layer. The waves were still cresting about four feet above the raft. Janice asked, "Does anyone feel like having some food?"

"I think we'd all better try and eat," Curtis replied, "and drink something too. We're sort of whipped from the bailing, and if our strength goes, we could be in trouble later."

"Yes, you're right, Mr. Myrick. Let's see what we have and go from there," Janice said as she began removing a provision pouch secured to the raft's inner structure. She withdrew small packets of concentrated food similar to what Bruce and Curtis recognized as C-rations. A water container came next, and the three survivors began a meal while the vinyl and rubber vessel bobbed and twisted in gusty winds.

When he had finished force-feeding himself, Bruce began fumbling in his pockets for a cigarette. The package he withdrew was soggy wet, and he started to toss it overboard but checked himself. Then he remembered his bag pressed between his back and the raft. He shifted and tugged at the small handles to move it so the zipper was exposed.

"Why, Mr. Ryan, I told everyone not to bring hand luggage aboard the rafts," Janice said.

"Yeah, I know, Miss Adams, but I couldn't part with my cigarettes, checkbook, and some personal items I've had for years that are in here."

Curtis laughed softly. "I guess we all have some things that we don't want to part with. No harm done, right?"

Janice smiled. "No, no harm done, Mr. Myrick. I lost my watch. It wasn't expensive but had sentimental value. It was a high school graduation present. I was just used to it I guess."

"I quit wearing a watch years ago after shattering mine working on an aircraft engine," Curtis added.

Bruce opened the cigarettes he took from the valise and began flicking the wheel of his Zippo lighter decorated with an Air Corps emblem. Finally, it produced a flame and he inhaled deeply from the cigarette.

"Look, I'm not used to much formality," he began, "just call me Bruce," and he extended the cigarettes toward Janice but she shook her head.

"Good idea. My name is Janice, Jan for short," she said.

"And I'm Curt for short," he added and they all smiled.

Cloud cover began diminishing except for a layer of thin cirrus streaks, the wind abated some and warmth became apparent as the survivors whiled away the passing hours. They began taking naps while one remained awake to watch for the other rafts and rescue vessels. Neither appeared.

"I wonder what happened to the others," Jan said at last and began searching the horizon.

"There's no telling how far we were separated in that storm. It was about as strong as any I've ever encountered, even back in the Navy. These Pacific storms pack a lot of punch, and winds are up to a hundred miles an hour sometimes," Curt responded.

"That sounds worse than some of those we have in Texas and Oklahoma," Bruce said.

"Yeah, you're right, and before that one ended last night I began wishing that's where I was," Curt said and chuckled.

"Do you think we're moving away from Hawaii?" Jan asked.

"Well, the sun rose in front of us, winds are from the northwest and I'd say we're heading southeast. We were going straight for Hawaii when the bird went in. So, yeah, I think we're east and south from the islands, but I'm not much of a navigator. I just work on aircraft," Curt responded and smiled.

"Charlie, Captain Dane, said once before ditching that we were about three hundred miles from Honolulu, so I think you're right. We're southeast, and maybe search and rescue will spot us soon," Jan said.

The sun began breaking through the fast moving, high cloudiness and added additional heat over the raft's occupants. Jan started to probe some of the pouches and withdrew yellow coverlets along with thin, vinyl posts and cords to erect over the vessel. "We'd better get these up for shade, otherwise our water supply might not be sufficient for us until we're picked up. There's also a sailcloth, but I'm no sailor. Do you think we should try and rig it?" Jan said.

Bruce and Curt both responded, "No," and began moving slowly about to arrange the posts and run cord through eyes on the coverlets. Shortly, the raft was shady and cooler and the three survivors began probing about to take an inventory of their supplies. Each announced their findings to the others, and a collective report indicated they had four days of food available. Water would have to be strictly conserved, they decided, but there was a supply of tablets to convert small amounts of sea water to a drinkable solution if the need arose.

The three survivors continued scanning the horizon in all directions and listening for sounds of approaching engines—either ships or aircraft. But neither came to break the stillness of a deep silence. A few sea gulls drifted by and hesitated as though inspecting the small raft. Billowing, white clouds began forming in the warm, humid sky above them and provided more relief from the blazing sun. Waves were cresting at three feet and the gusty breeze behind them kept their vessel moving along its course.

"Hey, folks! I saw treetops over there to the right just now," Curt shouted as they all began peering in that direction. Each one stared at the horizon for ten minutes as the raft bobbed slightly, but no one saw anything except water. "Curt, hold my hand while I stand for a better look," Jan said finally and pushed the coverlet aside.

"Okay, but be careful, we don't want you falling overboard from this great height," he joked and they all laughed.

"Hey! There is land over to the right!" Jan screamed. "It looks like a small hill with trees on top. That's what you saw, Curt."

"Great!" he replied. "I'll get one of the oars and try to rig a rudder to steer us that way."

Myrick leaned backward to lash the small aluminum paddle to the back of the raft, then wiggled it back and forth. "Bruce, how are you on steering watercraft?" he asked.

"Beats me, I've never tried it."

Curt laughed. "Well, if you'll slide forward to the middle, I'll take your place and try to get us in the general area of the land."

"You bet," said Bruce as he picked up his handbag and slithered to the middle section.

Jan sat back down but continued looking to the right side of the raft. Bruce raised up on his knees. "I've gotta try to see that good stuff too," he said, but he could only see more of the ocean.

"See anything yet?" Curt asked.

"Not a blasted thing but water. Are y'all sure you saw some trees or land?" he asked.

"I saw some trees over there somewhere. I guess it might have been a mirage, or maybe it's wishful thinking," Jan said.

A half hour passed. "Jan, you're not as heavy as we are, stand for a look at the trees again, please. Sight on me to tell how far right I should steer," Curt said.

"Okay. Bruce hold my hand, I don't want to get wet again," she said and smiled then reached out to move the coverlet.

Bruce, grinning, held out his hand to grasp hers.

"There they are, for sure! No mirage or wishful thinking. Curt, it seems to me we're a little too far to the right, turn it back to the left some," she said.

"Aye-aye, turning port. That's left to you fly-people," he said and they all snickered.

An hour dragged by and all three survivors could now see the fuzzy trees just above the horizon. Curt saw that he needed to correct their course to the right again. The land mass became larger and larger until it took on a thin, low line with an elevated middle where Myrick was steering to. Another hour passed and the trees were distinct. Now a smooth lagoon appeared to the left of the hill.

"Folks, we lucked out. That's an ideal spot to beach the raft, to the left of that highest peak. There's no ragged coral apparently, so maybe we can keep the raft intact while landing. Jan, maybe you had better stand again and see if there are any obstacles in our path. But I don't see any white water except on the beach," Curt said.

Bruce extended his hand and she stood in the bow for a moment. "I can only see wavy water ahead of us, no breakers or anything like that. It's beginning to look like a picture postcard," she said, hopefully.

Shoe Island

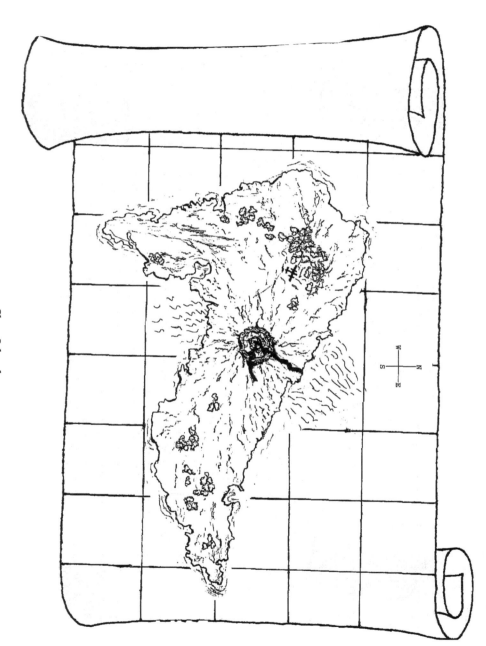

Chapter Four

Their raft came into the choppy lagoon as a strong breeze blew from their back. Curt steered with his makeshift rudder. Jan slipped over the side when water became knee-deep and pulled on the broken towline until the vessel almost touched the beach. Bruce and Curt stepped out and joined her. "Well, from here it appears to be deserted, but I suppose we'll have to look it over first to be sure," she said.

"I've heard about these small islands popping up from volcanic action all over this section of the Pacific. From the size of those coconut palms and short, spotty undergrowth, I'd say it's about twenty years old, maybe a little more. The underbrush is thicker near the hill's base," Curt added.

"Deserted, young, or old! I'm glad to be here and off that rubber boat. This is the best my stomach has felt since late yesterday," Bruce said and joined his companions in loud laughter.

"Fellows, I think the first thing we should do is take stock of our supplies and see what we have left. It will be dark in a few hours, and we need a place to set up camp," Jan offered.

"Okay," Curt said as they all began removing their life vests, "I'll haul the raft across the beach and up to the tree line as a start."

Bruce scanned the line of palm trees about forty yards away, picked up his bag and walked in that direction. "It looks pretty good to me in this area," he called after stopping. "Not much undergrowth and plenty of white sand. Shouldn't be very hard to lie on, but right now I'll gather some of this dry wood and dead leaves to assemble a signal fire in case we hear a plane."

"Good idea," Jan said, "and take some green palm limbs to place close by. They will create smoke and that's the easiest thing to see from the air. I'll tread out the SOS message with my feet down the beach a little way. Might as well finish these hose off, they have a hundred runs in them already," she added and smiled.

Then Bruce looked at her shapely legs directly for the first time. He glanced back to see Curt as he dropped the raft's towline at the spot they had selected shortly before. After thirty minutes the three assembled at the raft and each appeared to be waiting for the others to suggest their next move. "Let's see what our sea chariot holds. I'm a little hungry," Jan said and the others agreed. Then she heard a strange noise mingled in with the whistling wind but didn't mention it.

While they dined from small tins of concentrated foods and sipped water sparingly, they continued to probe compartments built into the raft. After all of the pouches were emptied the three of them looked over their survival equipment: a first aid kit, fishing gear, a large, sharp knife, signal mirrors, food packets, water and tablets to make small amounts of sea water drinkable.

"Well, with the sailcloth and coverlet material, at least there will be something between us and the sand at night," Jan said.

"Yeah, spread some palm leaves underneath, and it should be a pretty good sack with the life vests for pillows," Curt added.

"I think I'll gather wood for a small fire before dark. Might keep some of those crabs I saw earlier out of the sacks," Bruce said.

Curt laughed, "They're called coconut crab. The islanders use them for food. They can climb trees and crack the shells of coconut with their claws. I've tasted the meat and it's okay, just not one of my favorite dishes."

"How do the natives cook them?" Jan asked.

"I think by dunking them in a pot of boiling water, but I really don't know," Curt replied.

"Hmmm, I guess we won't be cooking any crab, no pot around big enough to hold them," she quipped and they laughed.

Bruce finished stacking pieces of wood into a teepee-style arrangement and lit some dry leaves with his lighter to start the fire. Then he took out a cigarette and lit it from a burning leaf. The survivors sat on the soft earth watching their fire grow as the last of the sun's rays sank behind a shield of red clouds in the west. Silence prevailed among them while they watched the dancing flames and listened to sounds of leaves rustling in a soft breeze.

Birds twittered in the distance, and a steady splashing of waves on the beach were the most audible sounds. Suddenly, a hissing, gurgling rumble filled the night as the ground trembled slightly.

"My goodness, what was that?" Jan asked and looked about. "I heard something like that earlier."

"I don't know, but it sounded like it came from the direction of that hill over there," Curt responded.

"Yeah, it did, and I don't know either. Maybe we'll be able to find out in the morning," Bruce added.

Quietness returned to the fireside as the they continued in lax activity. Jan looked up thoughtfully. "I wonder where the other passengers and crew are now and if they're safe. Search and rescue was notified before we went down. I'm sure the DC-6 marked our position. What's the reason for no aircraft today?"

"No telling, really," Curt ventured, "but at least they know we're out here somewhere and they'll be looking soon."

"I've sent the crash crew out many times to others in distress, but I guess I never thought about someone sending a rescue team out for me. Sort of a weird feeling to be on the receiving end of the stick for a change," Bruce said. Jan and Curt laughed softly.

As the three of them whiled away the evening, hundreds of miles away in Honolulu the other four crew members and eight passengers were settled in the hospital's day room that was lined with leather couches and easy chairs at Hickam Air Force Base. Medical personnel had checked each one thoroughly and found only minor bruises and scratches.

Charles Dane began speaking to the assembled group when their rescuers came into the room. "Ladies and gentlemen, I'm sure that each of you feel as I do—we're very fortunate to have been picked up so soon after going down, especially with that weather system we had in the area. I think it's appropriate to give these fellows a good round of applause to show our appreciation," and he held out his arm toward them.

The group clapped their hands loudly and some whistled while the Air Force crew smiled and did a quick bow. "They would like to ask each of us some questions and perhaps gain information to help them locate the others," he added. "Gentlemen," Dane turned to face the crew, "I can tell you very little, actually. We had the four rafts tied together and they were holding until the thunderstorm reached us. Then I think most of us were very busy just hanging onto the rafts. It became extremely rough! The fourth raft is similar to ours. The stewardess has on a blue uniform like this one," he said and pointed to Debra. "I think the two men with her wore dark trousers and light colored shirts, no jacket or coat."

The other Am-Mex crew members could add nothing to Dane's statement, and the Air Force crewmen asked each passenger if they could offer any other information. At last one of the Mexican ladies said in halting English, "I hear the girl call out once when the storm and rain come down. She say where are we, something like that. When the uh, *relampago* come I see her *barco fuera.*"

The Air Force crew looked at Pool. "She said when the lightning flashed, she could see the girl's raft was out away from us."

"Yeah, that is all I see and hear," she said.

Major Joe Fisher, a tall, dark man, the rescue mission coordinator, began speaking to the group then. "Ladies and gentlemen, while we're delighted to have picked you up, we won't be satisfied until the others have been found too. A search pattern began this morning and planes continued flying all day in an ever-widening circle. All of the airlines and shipping ports have been alerted, as well as each of the military services in this area. Every possible source will be looking for these people, and I believe there is a good chance they will be found soon. The weather has cleared in the search area. Good luck to you all and thanks for your help."

Debra stood and repeated the major's message in Spanish, then told all of the survivors that Am-Mex Airways had invited each of them to stay at a local hotel for three days with free rooms and meals to rest and recuperate from their ordeal.

That first night on the island was anything but comfortable for Jan, Bruce, and Curt. Their beds of vinyl, palm leaves, and sand grew cool quickly, and about every hour the trembling earth, hissing and gurgling awakened them. The darkness was thick enough to slice, and the scurrying of insects and rasping crawl of the crabs became acutely unpleasant.

Day Three

At dawn's first tinges Bruce sat upright and fumbled for a cigarette. He inhaled its smoke deeply and looked around. Jan and Curt appeared to be asleep, and he moved over to stoke the few remaining coals of fire. Shortly a few small flames emerged from the thin plume of blue smoke, and he added more wood to the burning splinters. While he smoked and continued to poke at the fire, Bruce could almost taste that cup of coffee he hungered for.

Jan stirred, turned over and looked at the fire. "Morning," Bruce said and smiled at the pretty girl's rumpled appearance.

"Shhh," she responded and pointed to Curt.

"That's okay, folks, I've been awake for a while too. I never thought about it, but sand can get pretty hard," Curt said.

"And cold!" Jan added.

"That rumbling over there didn't help matters either," Bruce offered, "and I sure want to find out what that is after breakfast."

Bruce stood and walked away from them toward the opposite side of the island to relieve himself. He then raked out a six-foot trench in the sand with his hands and began looking around to analyze more of their surroundings. He returned and Jan and Curt followed suit. At breakfast the three talked of their situation and how to improve their lot.

"I saw a good stand of bamboo toward the other side of the island," Curt began, "and that has a hundred uses. First, we can make a mobile blind for the john. Also, there's a large group of young banana plants. The leaves will be the closest thing to toilet tissue around." They all chuckled. "This island is larger than I thought at first. I'd guess it's three hundred yards wide where we are," Curt said.

"Yeah, there's a point to the east, and it seems to curve a great deal back to where the peak is. I guess we'll have to walk around the beach to see how large it is and what else we can find. I won't relish going over the interior much in my bare feet," Bruce added.

"I know what you mean," Jan said. "Just that little walk to the john got my attention. I suppose I should have kept my hose on, runs and all, at least they kept the sand from between my toes."

They finished breakfast of Spam, hardtack, and grape jelly taken from the survival packets on the raft. "Boy, what I wouldn't give for a cup of java right now," Bruce said.

"Oh, I was thinking the same thing," Jan agreed.

"Me too, but reckon we can't have it all," said Curt.

"Well, I have a jar of instant coffee in my AWOL bag, but nothing to brew it in, and really, we don't have enough water to use for anything short of a good solid drink," Bruce said.

"You have a little of everything in that bag. Mind if I take a look sometime?" Jan said and laughed.

"Yeah, sure, go ahead, since you don't smoke. Seriously, I like coffee when I first get up, and a lot of the hotels come up short on room service for only coffee, so I started carrying some a few years back. It's saved my life a few times," Bruce said and smiled.

Their conversation was interrupted by the rumbling and hissing they had heard throughout the night. "There it is again," Jan said.

"Let's see if we can pick our way to the hill and find out what it is," Curt began. "Then I think we should look around and see if we can find a water source. Coconuts are plentiful and the milk will keep us alive, but there's nothing like water when one gets thirsty."

"Coconuts I know, but what are those green pods on the other trees?" Bruce asked.

"Oh, that's breadfruit. It's similar to potatoes when cooked," Curt replied.

"Yes, they make flour from it in Hawaii, then use that for bread, cakes, and puddings. It's good and has a sweetish taste," Jan added.

"It's quite a valuable plant in these parts. The natives eat the fruit, use the wood for furniture or boats, and even the sap is used as a waterproofing material," Curt said.

"Well, so much for breadfruit," Bruce quipped. "Let's amble over to 'The Hump' and see what all the commotion is." Jan and Curt laughed at Bruce's reference to the small hill in comparing it to the Himalayan Mountains' "hump" made famous by aircrews flying over it during the war. They began trekking the fifty yards to the peaked area, but quickly found without shoes, travel would be difficult. Patches of thick vegetation and lava jutting up through the sand required much deviation from a straight line. And at the base of the hill, it appeared they would be unable to go any farther. But each took a section to find a passageway upward. After a few moments Jan called to Bruce and Curt. "Here's a smooth path, fellows. It looks almost like a child's sliding board."

The men went to her. "Well, I'll be darned. I can't figure this out at all. Lava is normally rough as a cob, and this looks as though a giant's thumb pressed down and left a smooth indention from near the top down to the sand," Curt offered.

They started up the pathway holding on to small plants in thick foliage and reached a level area eighty feet up. The rumbling hiss began and all three stopped. "Over there, that's steam and water gushing upward," Jan said and pointed to the left.

"Yeah, you're right. That's what it is," Bruce said.

"Aah, now I know how the path got here. Water made this strip before something changed its course in another direction," Curt said.

Hissing and rumbling continued for five minutes and the earth trembled underfoot. When it stopped, they resumed climbing.

"How's this?" Curt asked when they reached the top, thirty feet higher.

They looked at a three foot opening in the lava dome where steam and a slight trickle of water oozed forth. A pool ten feet long and two feet deep was filled with hot water. At the opposite end of the pool a path, like the one they climbed, sloped away to the sea below.

"Well, folks, our drinking water problem is solved," Curt said.

"Yes, and we can have boiled crab and breadfruit anytime we want them," Jan added.

"Are you sure that's fresh water?" Bruce asked.

"Yeah. There's a volcano down there somewhere that made this island, and with the water being so hot, all of the salt and residue are left in the earth, or that's how some of the smart folks explained it way back when," Curt said and they all snickered.

Bruce stepped forward and stuck one finger in. "Dang! It's hot!" he said and licked at the water. "Yep, no salt."

"Oh, we can also have cooked coconut for desert. There's a couple of them on the bottom of the pool," Jan said and giggled.

"I'll bet they're both well done, that water is flat hot!" Bruce said and shook his head.

"Folks, I think we should move our camp closer to the water supply. Shouldn't take much effort to move the raft, our bedding and the signal fire material down the beach some," Curt ventured.

"Okay, sounds good to me," Bruce began, "but right now I want to see what the other end of the island looks like." And he climbed higher on the lava dome to stand on the trunk of a small coconut palm leaning over horizontally.

"I'll be darned! The island is shaped almost like a woman's high heel shoe. There's a strip at the far end about a mile long pointing south. The beach curves back on the other side and bulges out at the ball part. On this side, it swirls inward and then out where the toe would be. We're camping almost on the toe section."

Jan and Curt climbed up to join him. "Yes, it does resemble a shoe," Jan agreed.

"Man, look at all of that jagged lava, and there's probably some coral mixed with it on either side of this peak. Folks, we lucked out and came in at the best possible place to land," Curt said. "Otherwise, our raft would have been cut to shreds by a reef."

"In looking down this side of the hill, I don't see any water paths, only boulders of lava and trees. How in heck can those trees grow in that stuff?" Bruce asked.

"It has small air crevices in it and soil down below plus a bunch of water, and that's all it takes," Curt responded.

"With all these barriers, I don't suppose we'll be exploring much on the west side of the hill," Jan said.

"From all I can see, there's not anything here that we don't have already, so I guess we just stay on the east side. I'll bet that lava would eat the soles off your feet going down that side," Bruce said.

"Yeah, it would. Shall we descend and get on with our relocating project?" Curt said.

"Yeah, I think we should. While you fellows do that, I'll bring the water containers up and refill them. I want to get some of the salt out of my clothing before it falls apart," Jan said.

Curt moved the raft closer to the lava hill as Bruce picked up the wood he assembled for a signal fire and carried it down the beach closer to their new campsite. Next they gathered their supplies and sorted them out on the overturned raft so they were easily accessible. Bruce then opened his AWOL bag and took out the cigarettes he carried in his shirt pocket on the raft. All of the paper was stained from the water and he knew the taste would be altered. But halitosis is better than no breath at all. I'll have to conserve them all if we're here for a long time, or I'll run out, he mused.

"Jan has been awfully quiet up there, do you suppose she's okay?" Curt asked after an hour.

"I guess so, but I'll go over and check to be sure," Bruce said as he turned toward the hill. A little closer he yelled, "Hey, Jan, is everything all right up there?"

"Yeeesss," she said, "everything is outstanding. I'll be down in a moment," and her voice was muffled by the rumbling hiss of steam and water.

Both men busied themselves clearing away small undergrowth plants around the new campsite, cutting bamboo for a blind at the john and assembling small lava rocks as a site for the campfire.

"Hey! Do you hear that? An airplane!" Bruce exclaimed and ran toward the beach with a signal mirror.

The engine noise was distant, he knew, but he scanned the sky intently to the north as Curt joined him.

"It's a long way from us, I'm afraid," Curt said while peering into hazy and cloudy conditions northward.

"Yeah, but that sound is very distinct. It has to be a DC-4 or C-54, and I'll bet it's on an airway out there. Let's see, this is Sunday the twenty-sixth and it's nine after twelve. Maybe it's a scheduled bird and we'll be able to attract their attention around this time of day when the weather improves," Bruce said.

"It's worth checking into. That's the first aircraft we've heard since we ditched," Curt replied.

Jan came back to camp and it was obvious her clothing had been washed. Her hair hung in damp, ripply strands. She smiled. "I heard a plane, is that what the excitement is about?" she asked.

"Yeah, it was far off to the north and we couldn't see it for the haze and clouds," Curt replied.

"From the engines' sound I think it was a DC-4, and it was going from east to west, probably into Honolulu," Bruce offered.

"Yeah, there are several airlines that fly them between the mainland and Hawaii. Maybe the next one will be closer and we can get a signal out to them," she said.

"It looks like you did a good job on wash day," Curt said.

"Yes, my uniform is gabardine. It washes easily and dries fast. And I noticed the water in that pool cools rapidly, so I just got in and washed me too. It was fantastic dipping into that warm water! I don't remember a bath feeling that wonderful in a long time. Bruce, your foot is bleeding. How did you hurt it?"

"Huh?" he replied, looked down, then lifted his foot and pulled the sock off. There was an inch long cut on the ball area. "I guess I did it running to the beach when the plane flew by."

"Let's get the first aid kit and do it up. Better keep the sand out or it could get infected," Jan said.

Chapter Five

"Folks, we're pretty well settled in on essentials. The water supply is great, a blind and slit trench for the john are in place, and the food source is better with boiled crab and breadfruit plentiful," Curt said. "But from my years in Honolulu, I know that the rains will start at any time, and they are wet wet. We'd better begin now and build a small shelter. Those coverlets and sail won't keep much water off when we're lying on the open ground."

"I'm all for it," Bruce said. "Just a few days into basic training, the Air Corps decided we should rough it, and wet ground for a sack isn't my idea of living."

"That certainly doesn't sound like much fun. How do we start? I guess the bamboo for framework, but what about a roof?" Jan asked.

"Yeah, bamboo makes a sturdy frame, then we cut palm limbs and lay them on until daylight doesn't show through," Curt began. "They will drip some after a while, but then you lay on a few more until the leak is plugged," he continued, laughing.

"Well, I think with only a knife to work with we'd better get on with it pretty soon. What'll we do, cut some of the larger stalks for studs and smaller ones for framing?" Bruce asked.

"Yeah, it's kind of tricky, but I think I remember what some of the natives showed me on tying the joints together without cord. While green it's easy to work with, but once it dries out, steel seems to be a little softer," Curt replied.

"Listen! That's aircraft engines out there!" Jan exclaimed.

They all ran to the beach searching the sky northward, and prepared to light the signal fire. But, again, haze and clouds were too thick for the plane to be seen. "It sounds like a DC-4 to me going back where it came from earlier," Curt said.

"Yep, it sounds like a Skymaster all right and might even be closer to us this time. I'm going to make a note of the hours for both flights, then we can look for the bird each day to try and figure whether it's scheduled. I have a pen in my AWOL bag, Jan." Bruce said, grinning.

Curt and Jan laughed. "While you two cut the bamboo, I'll try and mark a pathway from our camp to the beach. We all need to be careful about stepping on lava, and I'm sure none of us looks where we're going when engine noise pops up," Jan said.

"Good idea," Curt responded and Bruce agreed.

"Oh, be careful with that knife too. It's very sharp and I know that you want to keep all of your fingers," Jan cautioned.

Both men worked gathering bamboo material throughout a long afternoon, and as dusk settled over the island they decided to call it a day. An evening meal of boiled crab, breadfruit, and supplements from their survival rations was well received.

"I'm not used to this manual labor," Curt jested and began examining his hands for blisters and cuts.

"Yeah, yelling in a mike to inattentive pilots is a much easier way to make a living," Bruce chuckled.

"Boy, you two have grown into a couple of ol' softies. You should follow us fly-people through a hop on our winged chariot sometime," Jan piped up and they all laughed.

"What do you say we start early in the morning and try to get a shelter erected, Bruce?" Curt said.

"Yeah, that suits me fine. But I think after this afternoon, I need to follow Jan's lead and take a dip in the pool. I'm beginning to wish I could stand upwind from me a little more," he replied.

Jan smiled softly. "Oh, that water feels so great, it must be like the baths I've heard about at Hot Springs, Arkansas. You get out feeling like a new person, not to mention what it does for your clothing."

"Well, if it does all that, I'll give it a whirl too," Curt began, "and I expect there are a lot of minerals in it. That's the stuff that's good for you."

Then they settled in for the night wrapped in their vinyl material, and after the first few uncomfortable nights the water eruptions and other agitations disturbed them far less.

Day Four

Sunrise brought a start to their planned activities. After breakfast Bruce and Curt went to the pool when the water stopped gushing, put their clothing in to wash and shaved. As it cooled more, they stepped in to soak away grime and salt water residue.

"Man, this is really living," Bruce said. "Jan knows what she's talking about. A bath hasn't felt this good to me before."

"Yeah, it seems to get the kinks out of the joints and smoothes out the ol' hide too. You know, that girl is something! Who else would've thought to take her discarded hose and use them to dunk the crab and breadfruit for boiling?" Curt said.

"She's no dummy, that's for sure! And I think a lot of women in this spot would sit around whining about what they didn't have. Not even a hint of bitching from her, and she's always right there with us trying to improve our lot. Quite a gal!" Bruce added.

They pulled their damp clothing on and returned to the campsite. Jan was taking the husk from coconuts. "Hey, look at you two, clean shaven and well scrubbed all over. That reminds me, if I promise to clean your razor, Bruce, would you allow me to take off my beard, too?" she said and pointed to her legs.

He laughed, "Yeah, you bet, anytime."

"I thought I'd get the coconut ready for lunch," she began, "then when you got back there wouldn't be any delay in starting the shelter. I tested a small piece of bamboo, it cuts and bends easily. Oh, I went to the beach too, and you're right, Curt. There's a big rain shower moving along the western horizon. I'll bet it won't be long until 'Shoe Island' is going to need *overshoes*."

"Shoe Island. That's a great name for our paradise," Curt began.

"Bruce, if you have an American flag in your AWOL bag, we'll christen it officially and stake a claim to it for the good ol' USA!"

"Nah, that's the only thing I don't carry in it," he replied as they all chuckled.

With all three of them working diligently and taking only a short lunch break, by late afternoon their shelter was almost finished, lacking only the addition of palm leaves for the roof. It was a modified lean-to, freestanding, and open on both ends. The two sides were partially enclosed by a network of small bamboo canes on top of a sand heap, dug out to channel away the water runoff. As darkness approached, they sat back enjoying the evening meal and looked at their creation in mild jest.

"Well, I suppose we might have done better, but our plans are not to be here very long and it will keep the rain off. It's sturdy enough to withstand a pretty stiff wind too," Curt said.

"The only drawback I see is we'll have to duck a little going inside, but anything more than five feet up to the front roof line would be shaky," Bruce added.

"I think we did an outstanding job in a very short time," Jan said. "After all, none of us is a carpenter and with a knife as our only tool, it was bound to be something less than Buckingham Palace."

They laughed. "Okay, gang, it's accepted for occupancy as is, and first thing tomorrow we'll apply the palm roof," Curt said.

Distinct sounds of a Constellation going west just after noon had come to them, but they knew there was no chance of a sighting because of the clouds and disregarded a signaling attempt.

Jan held up her hand with three straws. "These are for sleeping arrangements," she said and held them out to Curt.

"The long one is for the right side and short one for the left. The other gets the middle," she continued.

Curt drew the right side, Jan the left, and Bruce got the middle. Next, they decided not to have a fire inside the shelter. Bruce began gathering wood just before dark. Soon he had a fire burning brightly outside, and the survivors ate around it speculating on the fate of their fellow travelers. "I just can't believe we haven't seen some signs of search and rescue after this long," Jan said.

"Winds in a thunderstorm do crazy things," Bruce said. "There's no telling how far away from the aircraft we are. They do a systematic search pattern. Circles, squares. Those can take a lot of time."

"Yeah, maybe tomorrow they'll get around to us. I just hope the others made it to an island or were picked up. One of the Mexican ladies seemed rather frail to me, and I don't think she would last very long in an open raft," Curt added.

Bruce picked up a water container nearby, held it up, then motioned to Jan and Curt. "Here's to tomorrow and rescue, but now I'm sacking out. The bamboo job has me bushed, literally."

"Cheers and good night," Curt responded.

"Yes, to tomorrow and a ride back to civilization," Jan said.

Day Five

The night seemed shorter than usual for the occupants of the new shelter. The day dawned behind thickening layers of clouds. Bruce had made small drinking cups from the metal food containers included in the survival rations. Now, he could sip coffee along with his cigarette. Jan emerged from the shelter. "Ryan, I don't know which you're enjoying the most—java or a smoke," she offered and smiled.

"Morning," he said and handed her the jar of coffee. "For me it's a tie, but you can try this one and if it's not a winner, I'll get a cigarette for you."

"Thanks and no thanks," she said and took the jar. Then she opened it, tapped out a small portion into the cup held by a basket-like twirl on a bamboo stick, added water, and held it over the fire.

"Well, I've got to have some too," Curt said and followed Jan's procedures.

After their usual breakfast of hardtack and grape jelly, the survivors began gathering and applying palm limbs to the shelter's roof. Two hours later they were satisfied with the coverage applied and sat down to rest. "I don't think we finished this any too soon from the looks of those clouds," Curt said.

"Yeah, it's overcast and sure looks like rain," Bruce added.

"Well, before the rain starts I think I'll break out that fishing gear and try my luck. The crab meat is okay, but a change to boiled fish might be a welcomed one," Jan said.

"I've wanted to walk the beach since we've been here, just to see what a little combing will turn up," Bruce said.

"Think I'll just lounge around some, but we do need a body to stand by to light the signal fire just in case. So, if you're both going out, I'll do that, okay?" Curt said.

"Yes, glad you thought of it," Jan responded.

"Here, I'll leave my lighter with you," Bruce said as he pulled off his socks and rolled both trouser legs. Then he lifted the edge of the bandage on his foot to check the cut.

"How's the foot doing?" Curt asked.

"It looks good, healing nicely, thanks to Jan's expertise," he replied and smiled, then looked at her. She responded by holding up her thumb and forefinger forming a circle.

Bruce began picking his way along the path to the beach and turned right at the waterline, walking along the shoe's toe. Jan got a small bamboo pole, attached a long line, took some leftover crab meat for bait and went to the left on the beach.

Bruce ambled along in the sand, stopping frequently to inspect shells and some small sea creatures that were unknown to him. He completed a semicircle until reaching the barrier edge where the peak began on the island's south side. Scanning from the water to the top, he thought to himself, *It's impossible. The western section of this dune will have to go unexplored.* He turned to retrace his steps.

Small waves were lapping over his ankles as Bruce stepped into the warm water and scanned the sky for any signs of rain. Then he looked down and saw an object just off shore that was foreign to the sandy bottom. "What the heck is that?" he asked aloud, and started to step out of the water until deciding the object wasn't moving. He saw red coloring for about six feet, then it dipped down into a sand covering and deeper water. Continuing to look down, he stepped forward and reached for it with his hand.

The object responded readily to his grasp, and he pulled up rubber sheeting about eight inches wide and an inch thick that was embedded with black cord. More of the material came out of the sand as he tugged it to the shore. Now it became heavier and more difficult to handle, but he kept dragging it until thirty feet of it lay on the beach.

Darn, this thing is heavy, but we'll surely be able to use the cord for something. Maybe I'd better go back to camp and get Curt to help me lug it around there, he thought.

Jan had just returned from fishing when Bruce walked up. "How was your luck today?" he asked.

"Pretty good. I was surprised that a little piece of crab meat would attract such big ones," she replied and held up three fish weighing about three pounds each. "How did the beachcombing go?"

"Hey! Those are nice fish, and there's one for each of us," he said excitedly. "Not much to comb on the beach. I did find something like a car's fan belt on the far side. It's so big and heavy I thought we should all take a look at it and see whether it's worth bringing back to camp. It has some heavy cord embedded in it, and we should be able to use that."

"Gosh, I wouldn't know what to do with anything like that."

Curt walked up then, "It sounds like a ship's belt. Is it six or eight inches wide and an inch thick?" he ventured and handed Bruce his cigarette lighter.

"Yeah, smooth on one side and grooved on the other. It must be thirty feet long and looks like it was burned in two," Bruce replied.

"During the war there were a lot of ships burned and sunk in this area. I'll bet that belt came from one of those. Let's go get it. I'm certain we can use the material in several ways," Curt said.

"While you fellows do that, I'll clean these rascals and when ol' faithful honks again, put them in and start the boiling operation," Jan offered and giggled.

"Sounds great to me, that crab meat is beginning to get kind of old," Bruce said.

"Ditto for me," Curt added and smiled.

Bruce and Curt went across the island to where the belt lay. "Do you think we should roll it up into a coil, or should we just each grab an end and drag it back?" Bruce asked.

"Let's just drag it. That thing will weigh a ton if we coil it into a roll," Curt answered.

"Yeah, guess you're right. I'll get this end, you take the other and we're off like a herd of turtles," Bruce quipped.

When they reached camp Jan was standing on the beach looking northward and turned back to them. "About the time I got the fish in the spa, I heard a Connie in the distance and hurried down to the beach. But the clouds are so heavy there's no way they could have seen a signal if I'd had one," she said.

"Could you tell which direction it was going? We heard it too but not very well," Bruce replied.

"I think to the east, but it's hard to say. It didn't seem as close this time as before," she said.

"This is Tuesday. I believe that flight goes to Honolulu on Monday, Wednesday, and Friday, then returns Tuesday, Thursday, and Saturday. Let's all sit down tomorrow about eleven o'clock and wait it out. I didn't hear it very well yesterday, but we were busy. It doesn't look like search and rescue is getting any closer to us, and this seems to be our best bet. Those clouds have to break sometime. Maybe our signal mirrors will reach that far," Bruce said.

"That's logical to me. Most of the airlines operate in such a fashion for these long hauls especially," Jan began, "and since we have the time, why not just have a seat and wait?"

"I think you're both right. Now, I have an idea on what we can do with the belt first," Curt said. "The natives wear a flat slipper made from a strip of rubber with a strap between the toes, something like a shower shoe. This belting looks ideal for such, and they'll help on this lava. So, tomorrow we can build shoes while waiting for the big bird to come again."

"Hey, that sounds good to me. These rocks really do a number on the feet," Bruce responded and laughed.

"Yes, I'll be glad to keep the sand from between my toes, the rest I can handle pretty well," Jan said.

Jan spent the remainder of the day boiling food for their evening meal, refilling the water containers, and bathing in the pool. Bruce and Curt worked on the belt removing some of the cord and trying to determine the best way to use the material. After they had eaten and just before darkness fell, Bruce called to Jan while she strolled on the beach. "Okay, fair lady, we're ready to measure your tootsies for a new pair of silver slippers."

She came back and brushed sand from her feet, then stood on the belt while he traced an outline of her foot on it with his ball point pen. He slid the pen under her instep. She jumped and giggled. "Hey, watch it, Ryan, that's where I keep my tickle switch!"

Bruce smiled in guilt and patted her foot, "Oh, sorry."

Darkness came swiftly with a thick cloud layer moving in overhead. The clouds appeared to be lowering as time passed.

The trio sat by a flickering fire making small talk as it became apparent an increase in wind velocity had occurred. "Well, folks, that rain that I talked about isn't far away," Curt began, "and I think we're in for a couple of day's worth soon."

Day Six

Dawn was long in coming after gusty winds awoke the survivors, then showers pelted their shelter. Bruce squinted at the firesite. The rain has done the fire in for sure, and I'll bet every iota of wood around is sopping wet, he thought. Dang it, no java this morning. Maybe I can scrounge enough wood to get a small blaze going, won't take much to heat that.

When daylight finally came, Bruce took paper from his cigarette package and was able to find enough wood particles in the shelter to start a fire. Then he darted outside and picked up more material to burn. Soon, he had a cup of coffee brewing. Jan lay silently watching him. Then she laughed loudly, "Ryan, I think that coffee is the most important thing in your life."

He smiled softly. "Yeah, it gets my attention most every day."

"Well, since you've gone to all that trouble, I think I'll cook a cup of that mud for myself. How about you, Jan?" Curt said.

"Count me in, it sure smells good," she replied.

After breakfast Curt began cutting the outlines of their feet from the belt and found it difficult to do. "Bruce, I think you'd better try and keep that fire going. What I had in mind for the straps is to make a hole in the flat part and run the cord through. But it jiggles around too much. I'll have to set a piece of rubber on fire and let the hot drippings vulcanize them in place. I don't think that stuff will burn easily, either," he said.

Chapter Six

Eleven o'clock came eventually, and the trio listened intently, but rain and wind were the only sounds they heard. After ninety minutes of waiting, they gave up and finished their sandals, then donned them with a measure of satisfaction. Bruce remembered to take wood inside the shelter for the next day. The afternoon dragged slowly by, and the evening meal had to be taken from their raft supplies. Night came again as rain and wind continued intermittently until sleep blocked them both out.

Day Seven

Bruce ducked out of the shelter at first light carrying dry wood. Jan came out when he had the fire started. Her arms were folded across her body and she stood close to the dancing flames. "Boy, that rain chilled my bones. The fire feels good," she said.

Bruce looked up at the pretty girl and smiled. "Well, you take the first cup of java. Maybe it'll warm those bones a little."

She took the bamboo stick and held the cup over the fire until her coffee heated. "Thanks, I need this!" she said and smiled.

"Man, I'm glad that rain stopped," Curt said, joining them. He glanced at the sky, "It looks like a nice day, and I think I'll visit the spa for a bath and shave, if you'll provide the razor, Bruce."

"Oh, yeah, it's in the bag, help thyself."

Jan laughed softly. "In the bag. I'm going to have a leisurely day, just sit around and listen for an airplane and maybe nap if it warms up a little more. Later, I'll do some boiling."

"Folks, now that I have shoes, I'm going to take a crack at going over the Hump and see what's on the other side. I've thought about taking the raft and trying to paddle around the barrier, but as sure as I do, I'd get into that lava and rip the bottom out. We might eventually need it to get off Shoe Island. Either of you want to go on my exploring venture?" Bruce said.

"No, thanks, I don't care what's over the hill," Jan quipped.

"I'll pass too, but if you find anything interesting, then maybe later we can go back and check it out," Curt replied.

At mid-morning Bruce went to the pathway leading to the spa and began his climb. At the top he started picking his way down through vegetation and swirls of lava. An hour later he stepped on level ground and looked back up to where he had descended from to note the position. Identical vegetation to that on the other aide greeted him as he turned left and headed over to the southern beach.

Curt heard the familiar hissing rumble, and got the shaving kit, then started to the Hump. He saw their survival knife and picked it up. "Think I'll open one of those coconuts if they're still in the water and see how a cooked one tastes," he thought aloud.

Jan was in no hurry to do anything this day. She went over to a tree to gather breadfruit for their next meal. A few crabs appeared and she slipped them into her discarded hose for boiling. Then she went to the hill's pathway preparing to climb up and await the spa's next eruption.

Coming to the entrance she heard Curt starting downward and strangely, he was mumbling to himself loudly. She waited as he groped in and rattled foliage along the pathway. "Curt, are you okay?" she asked while he continued sauntering and noted that his clothing was in disarray.

"Yeah, baby, ol' Curtish is jes' ri'."

"Are you sure, you don't sound like it. What's wrong?" she asked as he reached the bottom of the trench.

"Ya wanna drink a some grea' stuff, doll?" he said and held out one of the coconuts he had taken from the pool.

Then she noted his staggering walk and his flushed face as he approached her. "Curt, I don't drink. What is that anyway?"

"Coc'nu' juish, doll, coc'nu' juish. Cooked. Ha' some, is really grea' stuff."

"No, thank you, and I don't think you had better drink anymore of it. You've had enough," she said, turning around and starting to the north barrier.

"Hey, wait a minute, doll, don' run off. Ha' a drink wi' me, let's ha' a ball an' wait for our rescuers. How 'bout a lil kiss to toast th' day," he replied and reeled toward her.

• • •

Bruce guessed that he had gone more than halfway along the narrow southern section of the beach and had seen nothing of importance nor different from what there was on the east side. Then he crossed the island to the northern beach. It's all pretty much the same, I might as well go back. It'll take me a good while to make it over the Hump, he mused. At the hill's base the familiar geyser sound greeted him, and he started climbing from the point where he had emerged coming down.

At the spa, Bruce saw his shaving kit and the knife laying nearby. Stooping over to pick them up, he noticed a pungent odor coming from a coconut shell. He picked *it* up instead. "Damn, what's wrong with this? It must be rotten," he said and tossed it into the undergrowth. Picking up the knife and shaving kit, he moved on to the pathway and made his way to ground level. Where are Jan and Curt? he wondered as he approached the campsite.

When he reached the shelter Curt was lying on his vinyl covering face down. I guess he's taking a nap, Bruce thought and began looking around for Jan. She was sitting on the beach next to the lava barrier looking northward out to sea. I suppose she went there to keep from disturbing Curt, he thought and started toward her. Approaching, he called out "Too much solitude will get you down, fair lady." But she didn't turn or respond.

Drawing nearer, he saw that her jacket was soiled on the back and her hair was matted and sandy. "Jan, are you okay?" he asked. She turned and glanced at him, and he noted that her face was dotted with red splotches and her eyes were even more red.

"Is there something wrong, Jan? What happened to you?" he asked.

She didn't reply, but stood up suddenly and covered her face with both hands and began crying uncontrollably. He went over and put his hands on her shoulders to turn her around, but she shrugged his hands off and walked toward the water. "Jan, for goodness sake, what's the matter? What happened?"

She stopped and turned around. "Nothing, leave me alone!"

"Jan, something's wrong. Your clothing is soiled, your face is all red, and—are you hurt? Did you fall or . . ."

"Hell, no! Curt raped me!" she screamed and began crying and twitching all over.

Bruce stepped over and held her tightly in a prolonged embrace. "Jan, I'm sorry, very sorry that I left you alone. I never dreamed anything like this would happen. Take it easy."

"You, you can say take it easy. You weren't raped!" she yelled.

Bruce released her. "I'll kill that son of a bitch for this," he muttered and hurried toward the camp.

Curt was the same as before when Bruce reached the shelter. He picked up the knife before going inside. "Myrick, you sorry bastard, get on your feet! I don't want to kill you with a stab in the back, I want you to see it coming, bud!"

Jan came up behind him. "No, Bruce, no! Don't do this, it'll only make matters worse!"

Bruce ignored her and he put one foot under Curt's rib cage and flipped him over. Curt was completely limp and his face had turned a bluish color. His eyes were half open and his jaw sagged. Now Bruce saw that his breathing was labored and irregular, then noted that his clothing was only partially buttoned.

"I think the scum is dying anyway, but I still feel like helping him along some," he said.

"No, please. Give me the knife, Bruce, you'll only have yourself in big trouble when we get out of here," Jan said.

"What's wrong with him? This guy is only twenty-nine and sure didn't seem to be sick, but it looks like he's had a seizure or something," Bruce said after a moment.

Jan sniffed. "I think he had a stroke. We had a woman passenger once that looked similar and a doctor on the plane said that's what it was. Bluish color and difficulty breathing."

"Well, it's good enough for him after what he did to you."

"Bruce, he got drunk at the spa. Before."

"Drunk? What did he get drunk on?"

She sniffed again. "He must have gotten those coconuts from the water. He came down talking to himself and offered me a drink from one that he brought with him."

"Well, I guess the hot water fermented the juice, and that might be enough to get someone drunk. There was a shell by the pool when I came down, and it smelled rotten to me. I thought it was strange that our knife and the shaving kit were left up there too."

"It had to do something to his mind. I've heard that insane people have unnatural strength, and that was the first thing I noticed. He grabbed me from behind and I was helpless. The more I struggled the stronger he became. Then we fell to the ground so hard it took my breath. I'd taken my underclothing off last night so it would dry thoroughly. I couldn't move and—" she said as tears ran down her cheeks and her hands trembled violently.

"Damn!" he said and took her in his arms again.

He led her from the shelter after a few moments and walked toward the beach. "Jan, how long ago did this happen?"

"An hour. Maybe two. I don't know."

"You have to go into the sea."

"What! Why would I do that?"

"I read a book recently about the early Pacific explorers. When they moved out from an island, a lot of the native women were left with diseases and half-breed children."

"Ryan, what the hell does that have to do with me going into this stupid ocean?" she exclaimed.

"A gynecologist wrote an epilogue in the book. He said until those women wised up the tragedy would continue. Evidence had been found indicating they started taking salt water douches then most of it stopped. The sea water is like a saline solution, and they're using that as one way to induce abortions now."

Jan was silent and dabbed at her eyes as Bruce took her shoulder and turned back to the shelter area. When they reached it, he picked up the knife and walked off a short distance. Then he cut a length of bamboo from a stalk, trimmed it, and beveled both ends. He returned and handed her the tube. "That doctor said this is probably what the natives also used to ensure success. While you go into the water, I'll walk to the other side of the island and smoke. You'll have complete privacy, I promise you that."

She nodded and he walked away without looking back. Bruce went to the opposite beach and sat down in the sand.

He lit a cigarette and began thinking. Damn, why did this have to happen to such a nice girl. Was Curt just waiting for an opportunity to be alone with her? Why the hell did I leave them alone! It's my fault, I should have stayed with them. What if he impregnated her and we don't get off this blasted island? How can I help her? Maybe if I tell her the story of my classmate, Bobbie Pavkovich. No, I guess not. She killed herself and I don't want to give any food for thought, especially out here.

Bruce continued to ponder their situation, smoked a second time, and strolled back across the island. At the shelter he looked at Curt and saw that he hadn't moved. Then he called out to Jan.

"I'm upstairs, I'll be down shortly," she responded.

A tinge of compassion came over Bruce, and he went back to Curt. His arms and legs were spread at odd angles, and he straightened his limp body and fastened his clothing back. Then he put the life vest under his head and wrapped the vinyl covering over him. His breathing appears to have improved, Bruce thought, but he's still unconscious.

"I heard old faithful starting after my 'swim' and decided to put supper in the pot," Jan said as she walked up. "How does crab, breadfruit, and fresh coconut sound?" she asked.

"I can hardly wait. But thanks, it'll be dark in an hour or so and you're very thoughtful to do that for us," he replied and saw that she had washed her clothing and hair.

"Well," she said after a moment, "I might not look any better, but that warm water certainly did help my feelings. Now, if only I had a comb to get these tangles out of my hair and some makeup."

"You look fine without the paint, and I can help with the comb. It's in the bag," he said and they chuckled as he went over and opened the small satchel.

Jan started to comb her hair when the familiar hissing, rumble began. "There it goes again, and in about thirty minutes our meal will be ready," she remarked.

Bruce could see a sad and despondent look in her eyes while she continued the stroking. He wanted desperately to say something to cheer her and perhaps remove some of the hurt that remained. His mind, however, seemed completely blank, and he said finally, "Well, I guess old faithful has done its thing on our supper. I'll bring it down."

"Okay," she said as she looked northward into the last rays of sunlight slipping below the horizon.

The meal was routine and the two of them ate mostly in silence. Bruce decided that coffee would be a nice change and prepared two cups.

"Hey, the mud added a nice touch, but I can't help thinking if we use it all on luxury in the evening, we won't have any to save our lives in the mornings," Jan said.

"No sweat. We'll be off this paradise before too much longer. I hear the Connie roaming by every day, and pretty soon we'll get their attention with the signal mirror," he replied.

Bruce kept adding small pieces of wood to the fire, and as the evening wore on he realized that Jan was becoming less talkative. He could almost read her mind and he knew Curt's assault was now taking a heavy toll on her emotions.

Curt groaned loudly behind them. Bruce picked up a burning stick, walked over to the shelter and looked in on him. He came back to the fireside. "I thought maybe he was choking or something."

"I don't know of anything we can do for him. He's probably becoming dehydrated," she said. "But you're not supposed to give anything to unconscious people. He would surely choke on water or food." After a long silence, "Bruce, do you think the sea water bit really works?" she added abruptly.

"I believe it will. You know salt kills germs and cures a lot of things—sore throats, wounds. It sort of sterilizes most things that it touches on the body."

"What's the date?"

"Thursday."

"No, the *date!*"

"Oh, the thirtieth, why?"

"I was just counting, my little visitor, you know."

"Huh? Oh, that one."

"Yes."

Bruce added some driftwood to the fire that he had collected to maintain a fire bank and threw in his cigarette. "I think I'll call it a day. Jan, I'm very sorry. It's partly my fault, I should not have left you two alone."

"Now wait a minute! It's not your fault. How could you know he would do something like that?"

"Well, I couldn't, but perhaps he was just waiting for me to leave as I did, and maybe if I had been more aware I could have picked that up."

"No, Bruce, he was muddling drunk and half-dressed."

"Did he act like he was in control of his faculties though?"

"I don't know, really. He talked differently just before. Doll, baby, and all that. He'd never called me those names earlier. His face was blood red. It was over quickly, and he sort of stumbled away from me and fell before he got to the shelter. Then he crawled the rest of the way. A little later I heard him mumbling to himself. Gibberish is all that I could make of it. Then I lost control too."

"Let's try and get some sleep. Tomorrow is another day, and maybe our day of rescue," he said.

"Okay, maybe so," she replied.

They went into the shelter and took their places. Jan lay back and sighed heavily. Bruce folded the vinyl covering over his legs and adjusted the life vest under his head. Sounds of the ocean, insects, twittering birds, and crabs came to them. Curt groaned with an elongated utterance. Two gulls came into a tree above them and began a shrieking, fluttering squabble. Jan sighed heavily again. After a moment, "Bruce, are you awake?" she asked softly.

"Yeah."

"Would you give me a cigarette, please?"

"Sure. I didn't think you smoked or I would've shared them with you all along."

"Oh, I don't. Fifty years ago in college I smoked a little but stopped, and—"

When he lit the cigarette Bruce noted her eyes were red from crying again. Darn it all, he thought, the poor girl is crying herself to sleep and there's little I can do to help.

"Jan, I—"

"No, Bruce, please, don't say anything else. Thanks for the cigarette."

"You bet."

Day Eight

Daylight came with a clear sky and Bruce looked over at the still form of Curt, then turned to Jan. Her back was to him and she appeared to be asleep. He quietly left the shelter and stoked up the remaining fire embers. Soon he had coffee brewing and lit a cigarette. Jan came out of the shelter shortly thereafter. "Ryan, you dirty dog! That coffee gets me out of bed every morning, and I don't want to get out of bed every morning," she said and smiled.

He returned the smile. "Well, this is a good morning though, and we need to be up and at 'em."

"Aah, yes, up and at 'em. Crabs, breadfruit, and coconuts. All of that good stuff!"

Bruce laughed and handed her the cup with coffee and water. She held it over the fire to heat.

"We have just a little Spam, hardtack, and jelly left. What do you say we finish those off for breakfast? There isn't enough for three people and Curt might not eat again anyway," he said.

"Suits me. I'm burned out on crab. Guess I'll have to get the fishing gear out again," she sighed.

The morning dragged slowly by while a tropical sun began spreading heat over the island. Jan took a small piece of palm leaf and began fanning herself. Bruce wiped at sweat dripping from his forehead. Occasionally, Curt groaned but showed no other signs of life. Then the faint drones of aircraft engines broke the familiar sounds. Jan grabbed two mirrors and ran to the beach with Bruce close behind. She handed him one of the small, metal sheets.

"Twelve-thirty," Bruce began, "and the bird is going west. I wish the sun was a little lower so we had a better angle."

"Do you see the aircraft?" Jan asked.

"Yeah, straight north, a Connie at about fifteen grand, and I'd guess twenty miles away," he began. "The surface visibility is at least fifteen miles and he's out farther than that."

"Do you think they could see our signal that far away?" Jan asked as she continued to wiggle her mirror.

"I'm sure it's possible if we could get the sun's rays to hit just right," he replied.

The aircraft passed steadily from view with no change in the sound of the engine's tone. They returned to camp dejected.

"Darn it! I can't understand search and rescue. We never heard a plane or ship that first day. Not a living thing but gulls. Surely they looked for us," Jan offered.

"Oh, yes, they looked—just not in the right place," Bruce said.

Heat continued to increase, and a silent oppression settled over the island. Bruce walked a short distance and sat down next to a palm tree. He lit a cigarette and leaned back with his eyes closed. He didn't hear her approach and was startled slightly when Jan spoke.

"Bruce, could I have a cigarette, please?"

"Sure thing," he said and started to rise.

"Don't get up. I'll join you."

She took the cigarette and waited while he extended the flaming lighter. Her eyes were still red and now showed some swelling.

"I thought of trying my luck with the fishing gear again, but it's so blasted hot I'd probably blister," Jan said after a moment.

"Yeah, it's warm all right. I was thinking of walking the beach again from barrier to barrier, but I blister easily too, so guess I'll just hang around in the shade or maybe try to knock down some coconuts and pick breadfruit," Bruce said. "The john can use a new trench too," he added and laughed.

Each left shortly in different directions and the day continued to drag slowly by. They both skipped lunch, and in mid-afternoon thunder rumbled in the northern sky. Then strong, gusty winds moved across the island breaking the heat dome. Light rain began, and shortly thunder boomed and lightning cracked nearby. Jan and Bruce just made it into the shelter when a deluge of rain inundated the area. Runoff from the roof began blowing inside onto Curt. Bruce pulled him from his bed toward the center and hung his vinyl sheet up to keep the water out. Then he took out a cigarette and extended the package to Jan.

"No, thanks, not now," she said.

"I forgot to ask, did you have any luck fishing?" he said.

"None at all. I'm afraid it's back to crab meat for supper again," she replied and rotated her empty palms in front of her body.

Day Nine

Lax activity and boredom had begun to make each day like a rubber stamp. They had coffee and picked over their breakfast food lightly. Then she took a cigarette Bruce offered. "The next thing you know all of your cigs will be gone and I will have helped you deplete them much faster," she said.

"Aah, what the heck. When they go, they go, but we'll be off the island before too much longer and they won't be a problem," he replied.

Inside the base operations building at Hawaii's Hickham Air Force Base, nestled in among the other beige stucco structures with red tile roofs, Major John Fisher stroked his thick, graying hair. Then he went over to a podium and scanned the assembly of reporters and aircrew members. "Ladies and gentlemen," he began after a moment, "daily searches have failed to turn up any trace of the three missing persons from Am-Mex flight 755. Therefore, further search is abandoned as of this date, April first. I wish that I could add 'April Fool,' but I can't, and we can only hope that new leads will turn up soon. Thank you. We will keep you posted on any new developments."

Chapter Seven

Day Ten

Morning came for the survivors and brought little change again. After breakfast Jan decided to go fishing and Bruce began making a hammock of bamboo joints and cord from the ship's belt. When he became engrossed in lacing the wood pieces together he heard a snorting noise and his name being called. "It's not Jan, it has to be Curt," he thought aloud and walked to the shelter.

"Curt, are you awake?"

"Yeah, Bruce, something has happened to me. I can hardly move my left side and I'm starving for water. Would you please bring me a drink. I hate to ask, but I'm starving!" he said and Bruce noted that his speech was somewhat slurred.

Reluctantly, Bruce went to the storage area and returned with a water container. "What time is it?" Curt asked between gulps of water.

"A little after ten. How do you feel?" he replied.

"Rough! My head is splitting and I can't move my arm or leg."

"I drank some juice from those coconuts in the spa earlier or yesterday, and it put my lights out. I don't even remember coming down from the hill. You must have brought me," Curt said and continued guzzling water.

"You came down on your own. I was on the west side of the hill, remember?" Bruce replied.

"Oh, yeah, that's right. I had no idea that stuff was so strong. Damn, my head is throbbing."

"It was potent stuff. You drank it Thursday. This is Sunday. You've been unconscious since. Can't you recall anything after drinking that juice?"

"No. Sunday? I've been out three days? I can't believe it. Where is Jan?"

"She's on the beach fishing. Curt, there is a serious problem. Very serious! And I regret telling it, but you have to know. You came down crazy drunk on that coconut juice. Jan was there going to the spa. You roughed her up first and then raped her!"

"Oh, my God! No! I couldn't do that, ever!"

"Well, maybe not, but you did it!"

"God, no! Is she all right. I mean—"

"She's okay physically, just a few bumps and bruises, but her emotions are playing havoc."

Curt set the water container down and tears began welling as he turned away from Bruce. His body quivered and his right arm covered his face. While he sat looking at him, Bruce couldn't decide whether his feelings toward Curt were pity, doubt, or agitation.

Moments later, after he had composed himself, Curt turned back to Bruce. "Why did I ever think of drinking that crap? I'll never be able to face her again. Her life might be ruined because of my one stupid act. You should've killed me when you found out I did such a despicable thing to that sweet girl."

"Well, Curt, I'll be honest with you. I came here with the knife to do just that, but you were unconscious, and then Jan came up and talked me out of it."

"God! I wish you had! How can I live with myself now. Get the knife, I'll do it for you."

"No, I can't do that, Curt. Jan is right. It would make matters far worse. Two men and one woman marooned on an island. There's no way we, I, could convince our rescuers one dead man wasn't from a fight over her."

Curt was silent for a long moment, then began trying to raise himself up. After another attempt, he fell back against his bed and looked at Bruce with tears dripping down his cheeks. "What do you think that juice did to me?"

"Well, Jan said you looked similar to a woman that had a stroke on one of her flights."

"No, I mean before that."

"I don't know. She told me you seemed demented. Extremely strong like some insane people get. She's a fairly strong woman, and she said once you grasped her she couldn't move at all."

"Damn, damn, damn! What a stupid ass I was. How can I possibly live among human beings again after doing that?"

"Curt, I really don't know. I think you're being honest when you say that this was beyond your control, but that doesn't change the facts any. Jan is a very stable and fine woman—I just hope she can cope with the situation until we get off this rock."

"Oh, my God. Why, why, why?"

"We were not able to give you any food or water for those three days. You've had water, do you think you can eat something?"

"No, not now. But I've got to tinkle, could you roll me over on my side? I can cover it with sand when I finish. I'll never make it to the john."

"Can you move your left arm or leg at all?"

"Yeah, my fingers and toes will wiggle some, but they feel numb and tingly, like your foot does when it goes to sleep. I feel weak all over and my head hurts all over."

Bruce scooped out sand next to Curt and turned him on his side, then walked outside the shelter to pick up a portion of breadfruit left from breakfast. He returned and Curt had turned himself over on his back. The sand was smoothed out next to him.

"Here, you'd better try and eat something. This breadfruit was left from this morning and it's cold, but it'll beat nothing. While you do that, I'll go down to the beach and tell Jan you're awake. There's no telling how she'll take it, but I'll explain the situation as you have told me. Maybe that will help a little."

"Thanks, Bruce. I appreciate what you're doing for me. I'll never be able to make up for what I did to Jan. I just hope she'll listen long enough for me to apologize and get across to her how much I mean it."

Bruce went to the beach where Jan sat fishing. As he approached she glanced at him and turned back to her activity. He stopped next to her. "Curt is awake and seems to have paralysis on his left side." She looked at him again and tears welled in her eyes.

"He says that he doesn't remember attacking you at all. What do you think?"

Shaking her head, she put her face into the curve of her arm and Bruce saw the hand trembling. "I think he's telling the truth, Jan, and I've never seen anyone with more genuine remorse after I told him what happened. He said if I'd give him the knife he would stab himself. I believe he was sincere."

"Bruce, I've thought about this moment a lot. Secretly, I hoped you would say he was dead, and that's terrible! I don't think I can be around Curt anymore. I'm humiliated, embarrassed, and so ashamed."

"Jan, I understand the hurt, but you have *nothing* to be ashamed or embarrassed about. You've done nothing wrong. All of the other stuff should be on Curt," he replied, stooped down, and put his arm around her shoulders.

"Still, it's there, I can't help it," she said, sniffing and wiping away tears.

"Well, he told me he hoped you'd listen long enough for him to apologize. I know he's truly sorry. Just go back and let him tell you. Maybe that will make you feel a whole lot better."

"I can't! I'm afraid all of the anger and hurt will come out and then there will be all that tension hanging over us until we get off this island. Bruce, what am I going to do?"

"Well, we're here together for the duration regardless. I don't know the answer. There's certainly no easy one, I'm sorry to say."

"You're exactly right. We're stuck here together and will just have to try to make the best of it."

"'Atta girl," he began and sat down beside her. "I knew you had enough stamina to make the grade under the worst conditions. Jan, there was a girl in my high school class, Bobbie Pavkovich. She was blonde, blue-eyed, a very pretty and vivacious cheerleader. Sometimes she sort of flaunted her good looks around boys, but really she was just a nice little girl, working off some of her energy, and, well, hormones. One night after a basketball game, two cruds grabbed her in a back room at the gym and one of them raped her."

Jan remained silent and continued fishing, pausing occasionally to dab at her eyes.

"One boy's dad was well off, and he got a shyster lawyer for them. He had about six other boys testify in court that Bobbie was a well-known tease, and they said she led them on until the last minute, then left them high and dry. The two got off with a warning from the judge, and that was the end of it. I saw Bobbie weeks later. We had met on the street and she called me 'Bigheaded Bruce.' I asked what that meant and she replied she'd been flirting with me for months. Then she asked me if I didn't remember her hugging me after I recovered a fumble during a football game in the last minute or so to win it. I told her I did, but I didn't know that meant anything. I hadn't thought she paid any attention to the likes of me."

Jan laughed softly. "And then what?" she asked.

"I told her that I'd noticed her plenty, and would have asked for a date but felt she'd refuse, then I'd be embarrassed. She just smiled and said that was an excuse, that I thought I was something special, maybe too good for her. I argued differently, but she wouldn't buy it. So then I asked her for a date that night, but she told me she already had plans. I said maybe later or something like that. She said, yeah, some other time. The next day I found out she took a bunch of pills and died."

"Oh, that's really sad," Jan responded.

"Yeah, it is. Jan, I think now that she must have had the same feelings you have. But she was a flighty teenager and wasted her young life. You can deal with this trauma. I see that you have the stability to overcome it. You know, walking around outdoors, folks in Texas step in a fresh cow pile. Well, the foot isn't cut off, it's washed to get rid of the nasty part, you blow your nose to lose the stench and everything's as good as new."

Jan laughed.

"You're a fine and beautiful woman, Jan. The best part of your life is yet to come. A husband, kids, a nice home. As they say, the American dream is there for the taking. Just don't let this cow pile sidetrack it for you. Meet Curt head-on and look him straight in the eye. It will do wonders for your confidence and self-esteem. You have nothing, *absolutely nothing*, to be disparaged over. You were the victim. Remember that!"

"Bruce, how do you know that I'm not married now?"

"Well, no rings I guess."

She smiled and reached out to his shoulder. "Thanks. Glad you told me about Bobbie. Sooner or later I'll have to go back. I caught four fish about two pounds each. They're on a stringer there.

Would you get them for me, please?" she said and pointed to the water.

"Yeah. They'll taste good after several days of crab," he said and patted her shoulder as they stood up.

After Bruce got the stringer, they walked slowly toward camp. He saw that Jan was becoming nervous nearing the shelter and said, "It'll be okay, just hold your chin up where it belongs. I'll have the hammock done in a day or so, and you can use it to be away from us both at night. That'll give you a little solitude. Just take it easy."

Curt was sitting up inside the shelter when they arrived. He looked at Jan, tears immediately began streaming down his cheeks and he dropped his chin while his body convulsed.

"I'm glad to see you awake and up again, Curt," she said.

But he could only shake his head and wipe at the tears. Finally, he composed himself. "Jan, dear lady, thank you! And please, please listen for just a minute. Bruce told me what I did. There is no way that I'll ever be able to tell you how sorry I am for this despicable act. I've never in my life entertained a single notion to force myself on *any* woman, and I can't even begin to know why it happened now. I did drink some, but I've drunk before and nothing remotely close to this happened. I wasn't ever very religious before, but I've believed in God. I asked Him to strike me dead if I touch another drop of alcohol again. It has to be the reason for the way I behaved. I hope that someday you'll be able to forgive me for this horrible thing."

"Curt, I'll try. That's all I can promise now."

"Sure, and I'll thank you every day for the rest of my life. That is a solemn promise. Guaranteed!"

"You're sitting up, do you feel stronger?" Bruce asked.

"Well, yeah, a little. My left side feels numb and useless, but I feel better at least."

"Maybe it was that little food you ate earlier. I don't think the water would do much, but who knows, it might have."

"Yeah, I felt dried out when I first woke up."

"I'll clean these fish and get them in the pot for our next meal, I'm sure we can all use something besides crab meat," Jan said and left for the spa.

"You probably need nourishment before that's ready, Curt. I'll get some coconut for you," Bruce said and went outside.

He returned shortly, and Curt drank the milk, then munched on the meat slowly.

"I've started building a hammock of bamboo and cord from the ship's belt. Within another day's time I'll have it hooked together and ready to hang. I thought it might be more comfortable than lying on the sand. If it is, I'll do a couple more and get us all airborne again," Bruce said.

"Sounds good to me, and they might work out great. Too bad we can't hang them under the shelter for when it rains," Curt replied.

"Is there anything I can do for you, Curt?"

"No, I guess not. The only thing I can think of is a bath in the spa, but I'll never make it up the hill."

"Oh, I don't know, maybe between the two of us we can get you up there. Might be good for that numbness. When Jan finishes, why don't we try and see."

"Sounds good, and thanks."

Bruce continued working on his project and the hammock began to take shape. Jan remained at the spa for an extended period of time but returned just after midday with the fish and breadfruit prepared for lunch. Then, in the distance, droning aircraft engines drew their attention. Bruce and Jan ran to the beach with signal mirrors, but cloudiness in the north sky blocked out any sighting of the plane.

She spoke before they returned to camp, "Bruce, I think that Curt regrets what he did, but every time I'm around him, well, I feel clammy and nauseous."

"That's certainly understandable, and I'm sorry. Just do the best you can," he said and hugged her lightly as they walked. "I'll have that hammock finished later today, and we can hang it between those palm trees to the left of the shelter. That'll give you some personal space and maybe help some. I didn't mean to leave you with all of the KP duties and cooking."

"I don't mind at all. Actually, I like to cook, the only problem is the boiling. Next time I'll try roasting something," she said and laughed softly.

They reached camp and finished their lunch. Curt was able to feed himself and decided to take a nap when he felt exhausted. Bruce resumed work on the hammock and finally completed it. Jan had taken a long stroll along the beach and returned as he took the hammock to the trees for sizing and hanging.

"Ryan, you've done a fantastic job! The hammock looks great," she said and added, "but I weigh a hundred and thirty. Do you think it'll hold all this bulk?"

Bruce laughed. "Yes, that cord is like wire, and of course the bamboo won't crack or anything. Bet it'll even hold me up, but I haven't figured out how to put a covering on it yet."

"Well, I'll take it even if it is topless," she said, as she lifted her eyelids suggestively and smiled.

After Bruce secured the hammock to the trees Jan climbed on and wriggled about for a moment. "Oh, great! This is really living. I can sleep like a baby here. Bruce, thanks a lot!"

"You're welcome, and I hope that you do enjoy it. But it might get uncomfortable after a while."

"It can't be any worse than the ground. These joints seem to contour with my body. It feels almost like a mattress. I'll take it!"

"Okay, it's all yours."

Bruce went back to the shelter and Curt was awake. "The spa did its thing a few minutes ago. Do you want to try and go up there for a bath now?"

"Yeah, if you're willing to help me, I'll give it a fling."

"Glad to, and I guess to start, I'll get on your right side so you can hold some, then we'll just amble along at your pace. I think we can pull it off by taking our time."

After only one minor setback, the two of them made their way to the spa and Curt got in with his clothes on. Then he settled in and began removing items of clothing one by one.

"Do you need any help?" Bruce asked.

"No, I can manage, and besides, during my Rip Van Winkle stint I did both numbers. You shouldn't have to deal with that."

"Well, I'll be darned. I guess we wrapped you in the vinyl covering and couldn't see. Honestly, I never thought about it, but I should have known when you have to go, you have to go."

Curt chuckled. "Yeah, I probably wouldn't have thought of it either. Guess that's why hospitals poke that little tube in you the very first thing."

Before the spa erupted again, Bruce wrung the water from Curt's clothing, he put them on and they descended to the campsite without incident. The day closed after the survivors finished the remaining foodstuff from lunch. Bruce took out his cigarettes and offered them to Jan and Curt. He refused, but Jan took one and smoked it in silent thoughtfulness, then retired to her hammock for the night.

Day Eleven

The morning came and was similar to all of the others with little change in routine for the three. Curt reported no change in his condition, but did express an improvement in his disposition after the bath. Other than some afternoon showers, there was nothing to set the days apart, and they passed slowly away unnoticed and unchanging.

Day Eighteen

This sunrise, too, was very familiar for the survivors, and the only change occurred in the afternoon. Jan told Bruce in a moment of privacy, "I'm expecting a visitor today, and well, I, I don't have any personal items, except my slip."

"Huh?" he replied, then his cheeks began to redden. "Oh, I have an idea. I'll go up and wash my T-shirt. It has a few holes, but—"

Jan smiled and put her hand on his arm. "Thanks, Bruce, that's sweet of you, but I'll wash the shirt."

"Nah, it's too sweaty, and besides, I want to get a bath and shave anyway, I can do both at the same time."

"Okay. I'll go back to the fish pond and see about something for supper," she replied.

Bruce washed the T-shirt and carried it to the hammock when he finished. Then he began cutting bamboo for a second hammock. Several hours passed and he saw Jan go to the storage area for a drink. He went over and showed her the shirt. She looked and slowly nodded her head, then returned to fishing.

Day Nineteen

The morning arrived with a light rain falling. Jan was forced to come back into the shelter. Bruce started a small fire with sticks he'd stored inside. They had coffee and a light breakfast, then sat back idly while the rain continued. Just before noon the rain ended and clouds began to dissipate.

The afternoon dragged slowly along. Bruce was busy with his project and paid little attention to his surroundings. He saw Jan once near the hammock and later strolling the beach. Then he thought of Curt being totally immobile. He fashioned a crutch from bamboo and carried it to him. "I'm sure it will take some practice and patience, but maybe this will allow you to move around some without waiting for me to be available. Want to try it while I stand by to catch you in case you start to fall?"

"Yeah. Thanks a bunch! I'll give it a go. Sure will come in handy going to eat and to the john."

The two of them became absorbed in their activity, and darkness had almost arrived before they thought of Jan.

"Have you seen Jan recently?" Bruce asked.

"No, not in quite a while. Maybe you'd better check on her. It'll be dark soon," Curt responded.

Bruce went to the fishing place but there was no sign of her. He checked along both beaches for tracks, but all visible ones were old or led back to camp. Then he came back to the pathway leading to the spa and called out to her. There was no reply but he decided to go up the hill anyway. She was not there. He climbed up on the lava dome's leaning tree to scan the whole area. He didn't see her anywhere. Darkness had arrived, and he went back to camp with feelings of desperation that grew throughout a very long night. "Damn, there's no way I can get over the Hump in darkness. I'll have to wait until morning," Bruce said with dejection.

"You're right. You could hurt yourself seriously on that lava in a fall. Just hang tight, you'll find her unless she went into the sea, and surely she wouldn't do that. I think maybe it's that time of the month, you know," Curt said.

"Yeah, but she's sweating out pregnancy."

"Oh, my God! The poor woman. That's my fault. Lord, I pray nothing has happened to her, that will be my fault too. What have I done to that sweet soul?"

"Well, it can't be changed now. We just have to hope for the best. I'll go after her at first light," Bruce said.

Day Twenty

Bruce slept fitfully or not at all during the long, dark night. His mind was racing. *Damn, I shouldn't have told her about Bobbie. I could have been more supportive, consoled her more and encouraged her to think positive about possible pregnancy.*

Bruce finally dozed off but awoke with a start. He fumbled for a cigarette and checked his watch in the lighter's glow. Six-thirty. *It should be light in another hour,* he thought, then got up and went outside to stoke the fire's embers that remained. He noted their coffee supply was almost gone. *Hell, I can't worry about that now. When it goes, it's just gone like the cigarettes. Surely we'll get off this rock one day soon. Maybe we should get back in the raft and try paddling north to signal those passing aircraft.*

Curt began plodding his way to the fireside. "Bruce, you're up early. Have you slept any?"

"Not much, but enough I guess. How about you?"

"No, just a few short naps. I can't get Jan off my mind."

"Yeah, I know what you mean. Here, let me get you a cup of coffee. Dang, you mastered the crutch quickly."

"Well, it supports me and all I have to watch is the left leg, it lags behind with each step."

"Yeah, it does. Here's your mud. Do you want to sit down?"

"Yeah, and that's the hard part."

"I'll help you, hang on."

Curt sat down and started his coffee as Bruce asked, "What do you think about us getting back into the raft after we find Jan and paddling northward to signal one of those birds passing every day?"

"Well, it's a thought, but our chances for them to see us are remote at best, and if we miss, then there's the problem of getting back here, if we could find it. Somewhere else might not support us as well as we have it now. Too, we won't know how far to go nor do we have any way of remaining there until the bird passed if we did hit it."

"Yeah, you're right, but we've been here almost three weeks and I'm sure the rescue squad has abandoned the search by now," Bruce said.

"I think so too. In most cases they say if you're not found in a week out here, at most, you're a goner," Curt replied.

"We can talk about it some more later. It's getting light and I want to be at the hill's top to start down as soon as I can see."

"Okay, Bruce, take care and bring Jan back with you," Curt said and started to rise.

"Here, let me give you a hand."

"No, I need to do that myself and get better at it, besides, it's easier than sitting down."

Bruce began looking for the survival knife, but it wasn't in any of the usual places, and picked up a water bottle. Damn, Jan carried the knife with her, he thought and fear pulsed in his chest. Then he looked toward her hammock and saw the white T-shirt hanging there. He went over and took it down, removed his shirt, and slipped it on. As he walked toward the Hump he finished buttoning the shirt and tucked its tail inside his trousers.

Light was adequate as Bruce reached the hilltop and started descending. His mind began spurting. Damn, I shouldn't have told her about Bobbie. She left to spare us the grisly mess. It's Curt's fault for the trouble, but it's my fault for, well, I've given her an out. She just seemed so stable, but I know this has to be an extremely heavy load for any woman's emotions. Dammit to hell!

Chapter Eight

Bruce picked his way down the old lava flow and only slipped once before reaching the sandy floor below. He checked a minor cut on his hand and decided to look on the island's arch section first because it was closer. There wasn't a single track as far as he could see toward the shoe's heel. He hurried back across the island to the northern beach and there was a set of footprints leading from the area where he stood to the waterline and then turned back inland a short distance down the beach.

How will I ever find her if she's somewhere in this foliage, he thought as fear stabbed at his chest again. I can't check the whole area quickly. Then he turned to the west and went along the beach for about fifty yards. Yeah! She came back out on the beach here, he thought. Now, all I have to do is follow the tracks, that will narrow the search down some. He continued along the beach for several hundred yards and saw where Jan became indecisive. Apparently she couldn't decide whether to stay on the beach or move inland. Then she chose the latter.

In the light, spotty undergrowth Bruce could see occasional footprints on the soft earth. He began trailing her and thought of calling out but didn't. He felt foolish yelling for someone he couldn't see.

After a few moments Bruce saw a glimmer of something foreign to the green covering of the island's floor—light blue gabardine!

"Hello, Bruce," Jan said softly as she sat up from a bed of palm and banana leaves where she had been lying.

"Jan!" he exclaimed, dropped to his knees and put both arms around her. His heart pounded and trembling hands stroked her back. "Dang, I'm glad to see you. Don't do this anymore, girl. You had me—Curt and me—scared almost to death that something had happened to you. I—" he released her slowly, then kissed her cheek firmly.

"I'm sorry. I just had to be by myself."

He looked and saw the knife lying close by. "Did you bring this to cut palm leaves or something else?"

"I—I'm not sure."

"Jan, I believe that I understand a little of how you must feel, not knowing, well, about whether you're—"

"Pregnant? I'm sure you can't," she said. "But I've known since late last night that I'm *not*. I suppose the tension delayed me for a couple of days. Honestly, if I had been I don't know what I might have done."

Bruce grinned, unbuttoned his shirt, stripped off the T-shirt and handed it to her. He turned and started to walk away so she would have privacy.

"While you're at it, take a look at that aircraft over there," she said and pointed to the northwest.

He looked upward trying to see past some palm branches. "Where?"

"On the ground. It's an old military plane, probably a derelict from the war."

"Well, I'll be darned! It's a Douglas A-26. Looks like it crashed and they just left it. We might be able to get some stuff from it to make our lot better. I'll take a look," he said and walked away.

Bruce covered the one hundred yards hurriedly, and at the Invader he readily saw what had happened. The pilot touched down at the bottom of the shoe's heel with a clear strip of a mile before him. But an area of lava crevices was concealed and he didn't avoid it, obviously. The nose gear dropped into an opening and halted the landing roll abruptly. Most of the damage was confined to the front of the fuselage, but there was also prominent evidence of overall flak damage. Both main gear tires were flat, the right engine had been feathered before the crash and the left engine's prop was bent backward in the usual fashion of a crash. The cockpit's canopy had no damage.

He walked around the bomber to its nose and stepped upon it to look into the cockpit. However, there was a coating of scum over the window that kept him from seeing inside. He released the left section of the canopy, opened it, and recoiled in mild shock. The pilot had been thrown forward by the impact and lay over the control yoke. His skeleton was intact and covered by a crusty, deteriorating flying suit, while his radio headset was laying on the air deck. This guy might have survived if it had been the plastic nose model of the A-26, he thought. These all-metal noses with machine guns make more of an impact in a crash such as this bird crunching into the lava.

The bombardier was turned away from him, but Bruce saw a large gap in his skull near a damaged headset. He knew this man was dead before the crash occurred. There was an engineer/gunner on these birds, too, he thought. Then he went on top of the fuselage to the midsection. The machine guns were in place, and he scrubbed at a scummy coating on the turret's plexiglas. What he saw was expected. This man had been hit by projectiles passing through his compartment. Bruce could see that his hand still held the intercom switch. "He was alive and talking with the pilot before they went in," he thought aloud.

Bruce turned and went back to the cockpit. He reached inside over the bombardier to open the rest of the canopy. He looked for items to salvage. Two khaki uniforms hung at the back of the cockpit, and he slipped down inside and picked up three C-ration packages sealed in heavy wax paper. Then he had to smile. There were also two cartons of cigarettes wrapped in the same material. Next he saw two pairs of brogan shoes stashed behind the seats. All of this was routine for aircrews to carry with them into combat in case they went down, he mused.

Then Bruce saw a large first aid kit mounted on a panel behind the cockpit that separated it from the radio gear between the pilot and gunner. The pilot and bombardier were wearing their backpack parachutes and sidearms. Jan's voice interrupted his thoughts.

"Did you find anything interesting?" she called.

He stood up and looked out of the cockpit. "Yeah, I'm coming down and bringing some food. It's old, but it'll beat coconut cocktail any day of the week."

"Food? Well, I'm for that!" she responded.

He started out of the cockpit and saw the pilot's dog tags dangling beneath his chin. Bruce stepped onto the nose then jumped down to the ground. "I found three C-ration packages, and they're suppose to be good indefinitely. Crewmen sometimes carried them for inflight lunches on longer flights."

"Hey, that's great. I'm glad they brought them along on this flight—I'm famished," Jan said, then added, "Wonder what happened to the men after the aircraft went down?"

"I wish you hadn't asked. They're still in the airplane."

"Oh, my goodness! How many are there?"

"Three. The pilot, bombardier/navigator, and gunner. The bombardier was dead when the plane came in. Looks like the pilot and gunner were talking on intercom before. The gunner couldn't get from the rear section to the cockpit without difficulty and he was wounded. In fact, the pilot was too. Maybe that's why they didn't just bail out."

"That's sad. They've been here at least five years and no one knew what happened to them," Jan responded.

"Yeah. The pilot is Captain Kenneth Kyle. He was an all-American football player at West Point in 1943 and disappeared while on a flight to one of the distant island bases in the summer of '45. They awarded him a posthumous Congressional Medal of Honor."

"Oh, I remember that now," Jan said.

"Come on, let's bust these rations open," Bruce said and noted that Jan was carrying the knife and had a part of his shirt dangling from her skirt's waistband.

They went to a palm tree and sat down. The ration packs contained Spam, hardtack, rice, dried peaches, chewing gum, and a small package with four cigarettes inside. "Now, if we had some coffee to go with this, it'd be great. But I only thought to bring along a water bottle. I left it where you were. Stand by, I'll get it," Bruce said.

"No. I'll get it. Try the cigarettes and let me know how bad they are," Jan replied and left.

She returned shortly with the water and they both drank heavily. "Well, the butts are dried out but aren't bad. I have others left though," he said and extended the package to her.

"Thanks, but I'm going to quit again, so you'll be able to make what you have left last longer," she said and smiled.

"No sweat. There are two full cartons in that cockpit, wrapped in heavy wax paper yet. They'll be as good as these in the ration partials. Any port in a storm, as they say," he replied.

"That pilot, Kyle, what did he get the Medal of Honor for?" Jan asked as they began eating.

"Well, the war was almost over, it was June or July, '45. There was a hospital ship out here somewhere loaded with patients going back to the States. A Japanese cruiser came upon it and demanded a surrender because they wanted the medical supplies and equipment that were aboard. The captain signaled back that they were non-combatants and reminded the enemy of international law governing such," Bruce explained. "They didn't have a combat escort, I guess they figured it wasn't necessary any longer."

"Anyway, the cruiser fired a warning shot across their bow, and the skipper was ready to surrender to save the patients. About that time Kyle appeared, just like the cavalry of old, and the ship's radioman told him what was taking place. The A-26 attacked the cruiser with machine guns, as they hadn't carried any bombs with them. But that did very little damage, and the cruiser was getting some hits on the aircraft. So, Kyle then proceeded to make a high-speed run on the enemy ship and released two experimental drop tanks. One of the fuel cells missed, but the other hit squarely on the cruiser's superstructure and set it on fire. Meanwhile, the hospital ship was making knots and got away."

"Now, I remember reading that in the paper and hearing my parents talk about it. But I guess it just left me," Jan said.

"Yeah. I was in the Air Corps at the time. *Stars and Stripes* carried a lot of articles about the incident. The hospital ship's captain initiated the medal recommendation. He said the last they saw, Kyle was still in the area where the cruiser was burning, firing on it to ensure that the enemy didn't harass them further, and assumed that he was later shot down or crashed. They had lost radio contact with him."

"Well, now we know the story's end, but can't tell anyone about it yet. It's a pity he couldn't have made it to a base," she said.

"Yeah, one engine was feathered when he crash-landed, but he might have done that to conserve fuel after dropping the wing tanks. Possibly they were running low, or maybe it was something else and their wounds. The cruiser got a lot on hits on the bird," Bruce replied.

"I'm glad we found his plane. When we get off Shoe, they can send someone here to get the remains and carry them home for burial. Their families must have had it rough all these years not knowing anything of their fate," Jan offered.

"Yeah, I'm sure that's worse than getting the telegram," Bruce said.

"The telegram?" she asked.

"That's the way families were notified of changes in a man's status. Death, missing in action, or becoming a POW."

"Oh, yeah. Did you see the other men's names?"

"No, I saw Kyle's dog tags leaving the cockpit with the C-rations. By the way, they also had Class A khaki uniforms and brogan shoes with them. Crews carried those in case they went down or while visiting bases. The high-top shoes make walking easier and the uniforms were required on most bases, besides they're cooler than flight suits."

"For the military and convenience, huh," she said.

"Yeah. The uniforms are wrapped in plastic bags and look to be in good shape. The shoes were treated with dubbin, a waxy substance to make them waterproof. They look good too. I'd say the shoes will beat these clogs, if only they fit," Bruce said.

"Our clothes are deteriorating, that's for sure, but I bet those will fit me like a cotton sack," Jan replied.

"Well, the gunner looks smaller, so maybe not. I'll go back to the cockpit, get those items and close the canopy, then see about getting into the rear compartment, unless you want to do it for me," Bruce said and grinned.

"No, no thank you, I'm squeamish about that, admittedly," she said.

Bruce removed the uniforms, shoes, cigarettes, first aid kit and a flare pistol then closed the canopy. He brought them to Jan, then went to the rear of the aircraft and ducked under its slightly elevated tail section. The gunner's escape hatch on the fuselage's side was higher than he expected but was within reach.

He opened the door and climbed into the compartment. Most of what he had seen was now confirmed. The gunner still held the mike in his hand and had a headset resting on his neck. Through the tattered flying suit, Bruce saw where two pieces of shrapnel had entered his body cavity and thought, He couldn't have lasted very long with those. Another khaki uniform lay crumpled behind his seat, and a survival packet hung from a belt, along with a .45 sidearm, around his waist.

Bruce opened the survival kit that included sewing gear, vitamin tablets, a compass, money, maps, water purification tablets, and a knife. He checked the man's dog tags. "Well, I'm sorry, Harry Harwood, that you wound up like this, and thanks for the use of your gear. If we get off this rock I'll see that you finally rotate home," he thought aloud.

After dropping to the ground, Bruce slammed the small door closed and went to the front of the A-26. "I want to see what the bombardier's name is," he called to Jan.

"I'd like to know too," she replied.

He opened the canopy again and had to search around for the man's dog tags. "As I said to Harry, sorry, Steven Grumfeld, that your fate was the same as his and Ken's. We hope to get all of you back home one day." Then he left the bomber carrying salvaged items.

"Jan, the gunner was smaller than the other two men. You might size up the shoes and uniform to see if they fit."

"Gosh, I don't know. As I told you, I'm squeamish!"

Bruce chuckled. "Well, they weren't wearing them. Most likely all were just out of the GI laundry."

Then he showed Jan the survival kit and sewing gear while she picked at the bag covering Harry's uniform. "There's some parachutes in the bird, so if you want to make anything from nylon, like an evening gown, hose, skivvies, here's the tools to do the job," Bruce said.

She smiled. "Sounds great, and an evening gown is just what I need, like a bad case of hives!"

Bruce laughed and checked Ken's shoes. They were a size too large but he slipped them on his bare feet. "Hmmm, a little stiff, but I'll use them anyway," he said. Then he took out Ken's uniform and checked the shirt size stamped in black print just below the collar. "It's also too big. I guess larger football players grew where he came from," he added. The size indicated on the trousers' waistband was exactly his size. "Well, something that fits at last," he concluded.

Jan laughed and held up Harry's shirt next to her body. "It seems we were the same size. I have to think about the clothing, but the shoes feel good and I'll wear them."

Bruce went over behind the aircraft to change into the uniform and saw that Ken had applied his rank and U.S. insignias to the shirt collar. He removed them and tucked both into one pocket. I guess his family would like to have those, if we get back, he thought. When he returned to Jan, she was wearing Harry's uniform complete with technical sergeant stripes and Seventh Air Force shoulder patch. "My compliments to Mr. and Mrs. Adams on the architecture, and that's a nice fit. If they'd had uniforms that looked like this when I soldiered, I might still be in the military service," he joked.

She smiled and bowed slightly. "Thank you, oh kind sir."

"I suppose we should get back and share this luxurious find with Curt. He was very concerned about your safety before I left. Jan, I'm sure happy that you're safe and doing okay," Bruce said.

She dropped her chin and put a hand on his forearm, then looked up, smiled quickly and nodded.

They crossed to the north beach and walked along the sandy strip to the lava barrier making small talk about their salvaged items. "Well, let's cut through here and I'll show you where I get over the Hump. Should be much easier in shoes," Bruce said at the hill's base.

"Tell you what, Ryan. Pay attention now, and I'll show you how to get *around* the Hump."

"Go around, what are you talking about?"

Jan laughed. "That first day I went fishing, I looked over some of this end on the hill. There is a strip at the bottom of the lava flow where one can get across easily."

"Well I'll be darned. Why didn't you tell us?" he asked.

"This was my edge. I wasn't comfortable about being stranded on an island with two men. You never know. So, I thought to just keep it to myself. I started there when Curt . . . but didn't make it."

"You're right, of course. I wondered how in the world you got over that hill so quickly yesterday and just couldn't figure out why you chose to go that way. Over the top is a pain," Bruce said and laughed. "Lead on, oh wise one."

Jan smiled and led Bruce through scrubby undergrowth for a moment, and this gave way to a clear strip of lava leading around the base of the elevation.

Arriving on the other side, they saw that Curt had made his way from the shelter to the eating area and was drinking water. He turned slowly as they approached. "Am I glad to see you two, especially that you're both okay. I was sweating you out! Hey, where did the uniforms come from?"

"Well, we're glad to be back. There is an aircraft on the other side of the hill that crashed during the war, and we salvaged a bunch of stuff from it, including the uniforms," Bruce said.

"We have a uniform and shoes for you too. There were three on board," Jan added.

"I'll be darned. I guess there are a lot of birds strewn over these islands. The clothing change will be great but why didn't the crew take them when they left?" Curt responded.

"Well, these guys didn't leave, Curt. Their remains are still in the aircraft," Bruce said.

"You don't say. Missing all these years. What kind of airplane is it?"

"A Douglas A-26, or B-26 they call it now. And there was a large first aid kit. I think you'll appreciate the bottle of APC it had in it. Does your head still hurt?" Bruce said.

"Yeah, but not quite as bad as it did earlier. I haven't taken APC since I was in the Navy. Thanks for thinking of me when you found them."

"You bet. I appreciate the shoes more than anything else," Bruce said. "They are great for walking on this lava."

"The pilot of the bomber is a hero. A Medal of Honor winner," Jan said and added, "Bruce knows all about him."

"What's his name?" Curt asked.

"It's Ken Kyle. He had been an all-American running back at Army, and then was reported missing in action in July '45."

"Oh, yeah. He's the guy that saved the hospital ship from being captured by the Nip cruiser. I remember that well. The ship's skipper was the one who recommended him for the medal," Curt said.

"The same, and when we get off this dune, then the whole country will know what happened to him. But I wonder how his family will take this news after five years," Bruce said.

"I'm sure they will be relieved to know his fate rather than continue wondering from now on," Jan replied.

"Yeah, they probably will. I've read accounts from several families who have seamen missing and that's what each one says. They just want to know something definite," Curt added.

"Oh, I almost forgot. They had three C-ration packs in the bird. Jan and I had ours for breakfast. We brought you one for lunch," Bruce said and showed the package to Curt.

"It's been a while since I ate one of those, but I'm glad to see it right now. I wasn't looking forward to the next meal of boiled crab and breadfruit at all. Excuse my ungratefulness," he said.

Jan smiled. "Here, let me get the wrapping off for you. They really wanted that wax paper to stay put."

"Thanks, I'm that proverbial one-armed paper hanger, and on a crutch at that," he laughed.

Curt sat down and waited as Jan readied his meal. "I guess we forgot, the food is in cans and sealed packs. I'll get them all undone soon," she said.

"Thanks again. Say Bruce, here's something for you," Curt said and tossed him the small package of cigarettes. "Oh, and Jan, a present for you," he said and handed her the chewing gum.

They both laughed and thanked him, then went to get a drink of water and made a trip to the john while he finished eating. Then the droning hum of aircraft engines got their attention, but each knew it was in the far distance and only Bruce hurried to the beach with a signal mirror. Once there, he realized cloud cover to the north would prevent his signal from being seen and turned back to camp. When he arrived he saw that Curt had finished his meal. "Not bad, eh?" he said.

"No, siree. That was great! Thanks again."

"You bet!"

"Say, Bruce, what kind of condition is the aircraft in? Must not be too bad since the uniforms are in such good shape."

"Yeah, it's in excellent condition except for some flak holes on it. The bombardier was dead when it crashed, the gunner in the back was wounded badly apparently, as was Kyle. They touched down at the south end of the Shoe's heel, and when the plane was just over halfway along, the nose gear hit an area of crevices in the lava. That wrecked the landing gear and the nose plowed right into the earth. This finished the pilot off. He's still lying forward over the control column. The fuselage looks good, and the cockpit area is almost undamaged, just a few flak holes there."

"How about the wings and engines?"

"They're in good shape too. The right engine was feathered before the crash, the other prop is bent backward in the usual fashion. Probably the power was chopped before it made contact."

"I'd sure like to be able to go over that bird. No way I can make it that far though," Curt said.

"Maybe you'll be stronger in a few more days, then who knows, you might want to make the stroll," Bruce replied.

"Yeah, stroll over the Hump."

Bruce chuckled. "That's a problem all right."

"You know, Bruce, that wreck just might hold our ticket for getting off this paradise if the right things are undamaged."

"How's that?"

"Well, all of the birds making over-water flights carried high frequency radio gear to allow them to communicate over a greater distance. If we could get that out, maybe we'll be able to contact one of those aircraft coming by daily."

"Yeah, but we don't have any power source. Surely the batteries are dead after all these years."

"Oh, I'm sure they are too. But if we had a generator maybe there's a way to rig a windmill and turn it fast enough for a recharge. I think it's something we should look into. I've noticed we have a fairly steady wind from the southwest around the

Hump, and it's amazing the force of just a little breeze blowing on windmill blades."

"By golly, you might be on to something. I don't know much about radio hookup, but between the two of us, maybe we can figure out enough to make it work."

Jan came up to them. "I've rounded up more crab and breadfruit. Has the spa bubbled lately?" she asked.

"To tell the truth, I haven't noticed," Curt replied.

"Me either," Bruce said and added, "but I'll take them up for a dunking when it does, since you did all of the catching."

"No, that's okay. I'm planning to dunk me too, so I'll just wait a little while and see what happens," she said.

"Jan, Curt and I were talking about the A-26. He thinks we might be able to salvage some of the radio gear, rig a power system, and possibly contact one of the aircraft flying north of us every day," Bruce said.

"Do you really think it can be done? Oh, wouldn't it be grand if we could tell someone we're here!" she exclaimed.

Both men laughed at her burst of enthusiasm. "Well, it's a thought to pursue and beats all we've come up with so far," Bruce said.

"It sounds great to me! I don't know anything about radio except how to listen, but I'll help in any way I can. I'm going upstairs," she added and started to walk away.

"Okay, see you, and Jan, I'm very glad that you're back and in good health," Curt said.

"Thanks," she said and turned toward the Hump's base.

After a few moments Curt began, "What happened over there? I mean, with Jan. Did she say why she left or anything?"

"She just said stress had probably caused her to be a couple of days late, and she was sweating pregnancy."

"I'm certainly thankful she came around. Dammit! I'll never forgive myself for what I did, but I hope someday she can," Curt said.

"Yeah, I was relieved too. She's one fine person, and I think if any woman has that much vitality, it's Jan."

"Do you think she intended to take her own life if she hadn't, aah, come around?" Curt asked.

"I asked her that, and she didn't know. But she carried the survival knife for something."

"Good grief! Man, I never was so happy in my life when I saw the two of you coming back. Frankly, I prayed the whole time you were gone, and I don't think I've ever done that ever before. Not even during the war's bad days. I'll do more of it in the future, and I just hope now all's well that ends well."

"I think the worst, at least, is over," Bruce offered.

"By the way, did you see any kind of toolbox in that plane?"

"No, but I really wasn't looking for anything like that. The food, cigarettes, first aid kit and those things got all of my attention. Of course, the crew being in there was a little distracting too. I sort of felt like a grave robber, you know."

"Yeah, I see what you mean. I'm just vaguely familiar with the A-26, but most likely both engines have a generator, and the batteries will be inside the wheel wells. I'd guess the radio gear is stashed just behind the cockpit. The main gear didn't collapse did it?"

"No, in fact the tail section is elevated somewhat and the engine cowling isn't bad at all. The tires are flat, of course. The brunt of the damage is to the nose section. I guess it stopped immediately when the nose wheel failed," Bruce said.

"Great! Those landing gear doors will be easier to work with in shaping them to form a windmill," Curt said.

During the evening meal the trio speculated on the possibility of getting a radio hookup and if sufficient height could be obtained for an antenna so a transmission would be heard out to the twenty miles distance it must travel.

Chapter Nine

Day Twenty-one

As they had decided, Bruce and Jan left camp for the crash site after breakfast to begin salvaging radio equipment from the bomber. "Did you tell Curt about the secret passage around the Hump?" she asked while they made their way across.

"Nah, I thought I'd just let it slide. He might decide to try to make it to the aircraft this way. And, well, I think he's lucky to just be moving around."

Bruce checked the main landing gear doors first when they arrived at the plane. There was no damage to any of the four. "I'm going into the gunner's compartment now to see about a tool kit. Curt thinks it would most likely be there if they had one. Do you want to go inside or wait?" he asked.

"I'm squeamish, you know. I'll just stand by and offer moral support," she said and giggled.

Bruce opened the hatch and hoisted himself into the compartment. "Well, I'm back, Harry, and sorry to disturb your rest, but we need all of the help available, or there could be three more skeletons on this rock one day," he said. He looked all around the cramped space and nothing resembling a tool kit was there. Starting to exit, he decided to check behind the bulkhead between the gunner and the vertical stabilizer. There it was. The metal box was eighteen inches long, six inches wide, and eight inches tall. Harwood's name was printed on the lid.

The tool kit was heavier than Bruce expected as he started to lift it over the bulkhead and out of the hatch. "Jan," he called, "are you close to the tail section?"

"No, I'm at the wing tip, why?"

"I'm going to drop a heavy toolbox out and didn't want to smash your toes."

"Well, bombs away, Ryan," she replied and giggled.

Bruce noted that the box had a clip in the locking hasp and guessed it would remain closed. He dropped it and there was a loud clatter when it hit the sand below. Then he climbed out and followed the parcel down. The box contained most of the usual items: open-end wrenches, pliers, screwdrivers, socket wrenches, a few loose nuts and bolts, a ball-peen hammer, and most importantly, a pair of metal shears.

"I guess the next thing to do is go into the cockpit and try to find the right transmitter and receiver. I wish I'd talked with the electronic technicians at work more about radio equipment. I use it every day yet know so little about it," Bruce said.

"I know what you mean. I can press a mike button and that's about it for me," Jan replied.

Bruce entered the cockpit and began looking over two rows of radio equipment just forward of the bomb bay. He recognized one receiver used to pick up radio beacons marking an airway. Then he saw another set on 3023.5 kilocycles, the emergency frequency most traffic facilities continuously monitor in the States. "Now, all I have to do is find a matching transmitter. All receivers on one side, transmitter on the other," he said to himself.

As he exited the cockpit Jan called to him, "Did you find what you were looking for yet?"

"Yeah, got 'em both. But dumb me, I forgot to bring any tools up here to remove them."

She giggled, "Well, I know as much about tools as I do radios, don't know one from another or I'd get them for you."

"Aah, no sweat. It'll take a socket wrench to remove the bolts holding the sets onto the racks. I'll have them out shortly."

He selected three different sizes of sockets, got a handle from the tool kit and went back into the aircraft. He withdrew the transmitter with a dangling plug and set it on the fuselage behind the cockpit. A little later he came out with a receiver unit and brought it down to where Jan waited. He stooped over to set it down, and when he raised back up she was right in front of him. They stood looking at each other for a long moment, and Bruce realized this was the first time he had ever stared deeply into her beautiful eyes. She continued to scan his face expressionless. Both of them smiled, he patted her shoulder and went back for the transmitter.

Bruce carried the transmitter unit down and placed it next to the receiver then wiped the moisture collecting on his forehead.

"We lucked out on the antenna, it's mounted just above the radio gear and will be easy to remove," he said.

"Is that it, the pointed thing?"

"Yeah, holding the cable hooked to the vertical stabilizer. I'll get those off now, then we'll look for the battery and generator."

"Well, it seems to me, *you're* doing all of the work and *I'm* standing around like a lady of leisure."

"Just stand by, Miss Adams. *We* have to get the stuff back to camp."

"Okay, Mr. Ryan, whatever you say," she replied and smiled.

Bruce went back onto the aircraft and removed the antenna cable from the rudder fin first. Next he worked on the fuselage and the antenna. Soon the material was all disconnected and he brought it down to the ground. He handed Jan a pair of thin, black leather gloves bearing the Air Corps emblem. "I found these laying on the air deck. They will help when you start carrying these metal objects around by hand," he said and chuckled.

"So they will, thanks."

"While I check the engine nacelle on the other side, look inside this one and see if you can spot anything resembling a battery, please," he said and went to the far side of the bomber.

After a moment she called out, "Yes, there's one here, but it looks corroded."

"Okay, there's one in this wheel well, and it has some corrosion too, but at least we have them," Bruce replied and went to the toolbox for a socket wrench.

When he had removed the batteries, Bruce took a pair of pliers and touched their handles to the terminals. There was no spark at all.

"They're both dead," he said while removing caps from the water wells. "And they've been dry for a long time. Maybe a drink from the spa will revive them."

"Bruce, these things are heavy. How will we get them *and* the radio equipment back to camp?" Jan asked.

"Well, I thought once we get the gear doors off, the batteries and radios could be placed on those. We'll also need a lot of wiring from the bird, so I'll hook that to the doors and use them like a slide. Should work okay, don't you think?"

"Man, that's pretty smart. Yes, it will work," she said.

"I'm not such a smarty. I don't have a clue where the generator is. It wasn't in either wheel well. Did you see anything resembling one anywhere?" he asked.

"Gosh, I don't think so, but I'm not sure what they look like."

He laughed. "It has to be on the engine somewhere," Bruce said and he began prying at several cowl flaps to see inside the engine covering. After fifteen minutes without success, he stopped.

They decided to take a lunch break next. Jan found two small coconuts, and both drank heavily from the water bottle they brought.

"Bruce," she began as he sat smoking after eating, "how did that pilot get the bomber this far without hitting a palm tree?"

"You know, I thought about that too. These trees here are smaller and shorter than those closer to camp. Most likely these weren't all here then. He must have seen a fairly long, clear strip to attempt a landing, otherwise he would've set it down on the beach, probably with the gear up."

"That sounds logical to me, and he did a good job until the lava got in his way."

They sat for a few more moments and Jan refused his offer of a cigarette. "Okay, sarge, let's see if we can get the gear doors off that bird," Bruce said.

Jan brushed at a chevron on her sleeve and smiled. "All right, let's go. Hey! Listen. There's the Connie going by right on time, it must be about ten-thirty. If only we had the radio working."

"Yeah. For the record, it's twenty after ten, Pacific Time," he replied after checking his watch.

After more than an hour of hammering and cutting on the metal hinges, all four gear well doors were laid out on the ground and Bruce placed the equipment on them. "One more trip inside to get the wire and we're finished," he said. Then he took a pair of snips from the tool kit and went inside the cockpit. Fifteen minutes later he emerged carrying several strips of multi-colored wire about eight feet long encased in clear plastic. "One good thing about aircraft wiring is, they bundle it together in thick strands, so there's no fumbling around to get at it," he said.

Once Bruce had some wire attached firmly on two of the doors, they started towing the material toward camp. "I think we should get on the beach as quickly as possible. The undergrowth makes it difficult to pull the doors without a lot of weaving," Jan said.

"Yeah, you're right, let's cut across now," he replied.

As they approached the pathway leading around the hill Jan said, "You know, we can't drag these doors across that lava. Our equipment would be in the ocean fast. What do we do, stop and carry each item over separately?"

"I hadn't thought about it, but you're right. Let's just pull them up as close as we can, then I'll take them over to the other side, it's only forty yards or so, shouldn't be much of a job," he said.

"The gloves you gave me will help. I'll carry some of the lighter things, that will save you a few steps," Jan offered.

"Okay, thanks, but don't try the heavy ones. We don't want the queen of Shoe Island to strip a gear doing manual labor."

She laughed. "Yeah, I'm a queen all right, and you're my knight in shining armor."

Bruce grinned. "Speaking of armor, we'll need to round up some of those armored critters for dinner. I've just about worked up my appetite. If you will, why don't you work on that while I carry this stuff by the Hump. Really, I'd forgotten about Curt. He probably skipped lunch."

"Oh, gosh, I had too. Okay, you're on, I'll do it."

"You are a real queen, thanks!"

In an hour, Bruce had finished his work and all of the gear was assembled at the campsite. Jan had gathered crab and breadfruit, then left for the spa to boil them. "Curt, I didn't realize it would take us all day to get this little bit of stuff here. How did you make out at lunch?" Bruce asked.

"I had coconut cocktail and an APC," he answered as he laughed. "No sweat, I knew it would take a great deal of time. No luck on the generator, huh?"

"No, it wasn't in either wheel well, so I thought to talk with you some more first. I tried spotting it by lifting the cowl flaps up, but couldn't see much of anything that way."

"I should have thought about it more. The generator will be mounted at the back of the engine, well behind the cowl flaps. Look for the fire extinguisher port somewhere on the fuselage. It'll have a label on the door. A lot of them have a small ax stashed with the fire bottle. You can cut through the cowling with that and not have to remove the entire engine covering to get to the gen."

After they had eaten, Curt went through the tool kit to see what was available, and he found some alligator clips. "These will secure the wires for a better connection to the battery," he said. Then checking over the batteries, he placed the pliers loosely over the terminal posts and skewed them around to remove corrosion. Next he looked into the water wells. "There's no way to tell if these will take a charge, assuming we can get a hookup, but they do need water and the sooner the better."

"I'll get the bottle and fill both right now," Bruce said and hurried to the spa.

Night fell as the trio sat at the fireside making idle conversation. Jan mentioned to Curt they had found a passage around the Hump and he expressed delight about it being easier to get to the bomber for additional material. Then he tinkered with the radio gear. "We probably should set the equipment up inside the shelter to keep it dry. I think we have everything needed to make the units work if we can get those batteries charged. Oh! We need a mike and earphones too, so you might check on those when you go back for the gen, Bruce. By the way, that rascal is going to be heavy," he said.

"Okay, I'll carry a gear door to bring it back on, and Kyle's headset looks good. I'll get that next trip."

The survivors retired for the day with thoughts of rescue dancing in their minds. Bruce was now in a hammock, but Curt decided against trying to sleep in one because of the possibility of falling, so he remained in the shelter. At some time during the night Bruce awoke from a sound sleep and heard Curt making noises similar to those he made while he was in a coma. The noise stopped shortly, however, and he resumed his sleep.

Chapter Ten

Day Twenty-two

Heavy cloud cover held back daylight for an extended amount of time and Bruce worried about rainfall hampering his plans of going back to the crash site. Finally, it was light enough to begin preparations. He had coffee, coconut, and a cigarette just before starting to leave. Curt ambled up and joined him at the fire. Bruce noted that he looked flaccid and tired. "Here, let me get you a cup of our best mud, it'll do wonders for you," he said.

"Wonders is just what I need about now," Curt chuckled.

Bruce heated the coffee and handed it to him. What type wrench do you suppose I'll need to get the generator off?"

"It's hard to say, I'd carry the whole litter with me if I were you. No sense in having to come all the way back for a socket or something like that. I'm guessing it will be mounted on a shelf-like device with small anchor bolts holding it."

"Okay, that's what I'll do. Curt, you feel rough don't you?"

"Well, I've felt better. The APC helps, and I'm gonna take one shortly, That should do the trick. Be careful taking that generator out and don't get hurt."

"Good morning. Looks like I'm the procrastinator today," Jan said as she came up to the fireside.

"Morning," Bruce responded and handed her the bamboo cane holding a cup of coffee that he had already mixed.

"Looks like a lazy morning," Curt said, then added, "that's one thing about this paradise, none of us has to hurry to do anything."

They all laughed while Jan heated her coffee. "Do you want to go back to the bomber with me today, Jan?" Bruce asked.

"No, not right away. I want to get some of those bamboo shoots to cook, and of course, more crab and breadfruit. We can all stand a change in our diet, I think," she said.

"Bamboo shoots, to eat?" Bruce questioned.

"Yes, I've read that they are eaten in a lot of ways, and supposedly, they're good for you," she said.

"Yeah, the natives in Hawaii eat them regularly," Curt added.

Bruce gathered some cord from the ship's belt to use with the gear door, then picked up the tool kit. "Well, I guess I'm off, folks. I'll be back with a generator sometime, but I gotta find it first."

They bade him farewell and good hunting, and he left. He went around the Hump and decided to rig the slide to carry the heavy toolbox.

The aircraft seemed gloomier with heavy clouds looming above, and Bruce hesitated to begin work. Somehow, this still seems like grave robbing to me, but these guys are gone—no changing that, and if we can help ourselves with this equipment I'm sure they wouldn't mind, he decided. The left engine is closer, so I'll do that one. But first, I'd better do as Curt said and look for the fire extinguisher port. An ax will make it simpler to get to the generator, that's for sure.

Bruce found the port quickly, and there was a small, all-metal hatchet clipped to the inner side. He then went to the engine and began splitting the housing back of the cowl flaps. After an hour of chopping aluminum, the generator was fully exposed on a pallet just back of and beneath the engine. Now all I have to do is get those anchor bolts loose and take the rascal out. But first, I'd better do something with this jagged covering. Sure as the world, I'll rip my arms open or worse, he thought.

He took the hatchet and pliers and folded the engine's metal covering back from his work area. Then he began unscrewing the anchor bolts to free his prize. Once this was complete, he began trying to release the shaft's gear from a corresponding one attached to the engine's crankshaft. But it remained stationary. Dang! I should've known the gears had a housing to cover them to keep the grease somewhat in place, he thought. Two swings with the hammer sent the small cover flying, and the generator lifted off easily.

"Curt was right! This rascal is heavy," he said to himself while straining hard to lift the generator out of the engine housing. "It's gotta weigh forty pounds at least," he continued while carrying it to the gear door nearby. Then he decided to take a smoke break, but looked at the cockpit and saw that he had left one of the two canopy panels open yesterday. The least I can do is keep rain off you guys, he mused. He climbed back on the bomber to close the panel, but instead he went inside and picked up Ken's headset with the mike attached.

After climbing down, he sat next to the left engine and lit a cigarette. His watch showed he had been there two and a half hours, and he decided to rest and finish smoking before starting back to camp. While sitting, he leaned against the engine and closed his eyes. There was no sound, but Bruce sensed someone's presence and looked up. Jan stood close by smiling at him. "Oh, I'm sorry to disturb your reverie," she said.

"Aah, I'm just goofing off," he chuckled. "Want to join me for a smoke?"

"No, thanks, I'll pass," she replied and continued smiling at him.

Bruce kept looking at her and realized again what a strikingly beautiful woman she was, even attired in a man's military uniform. He smiled at her, snuffed out his cigarette in the sand and started over to the pile of equipment. "Well, we now have a generator, a mike, and earphones to go with the batteries and radio gear. All that's left is to get them working."

"That's great. Let's hope we can," she said. Jan went over to him and began ruffling his hair with her hand. "I'll bet that was hard work getting the generator out."

"Nah, it wasn't too bad, just slow. I didn't really know what I was doing."

Jan laughed, ruffled his hair some more and turned away. "You did a good job, now it's all up to Curt."

Bruce placed all of the equipment on the gear door and they started walking slowly toward the Hump with the slide trailing behind. "How did the cooking go, especially the bamboo shoots?" he asked after a moment.

"Pretty good, actually, but they would be much better with just a dab of seasoning. Even a little sea water would help, but it's *almost impossible* to get those old hose to hold water," she jested.

"Hey, that reminds me. Yesterday I saw a GI canteen in the cockpit, and I'll bet there's a cup inside that canvas covering. Hang on a minute and I'll get it," he said and turned back to the bomber.

He returned shortly holding an aluminum canteen in one hand and a cup that fit over the bottom section. A small chain securing the black plastic cap clinked as he worked with it. "The cover was shot, so I pulled it off, but I can't budge this top with my hands. I can hear liquid splashing inside, and there's no telling what they had in it. The cup is a little corroded, but a dunking in the spa will clean it good and it'll make a great cooking pot, for shoots or whatever."

Jan reached for the cup. "Yeah, a good sand scrubbing and a dunk will fix it just right. Are you going to try pliers on the top of .the canteen?"

"Yep, gotta see what ol' Ken was drinking," he said and took pliers from the tool kit. The top crumbled when he applied the tool and Bruce held the canteen up to his a nose. "Whew! Man, that's raunchy! It had to be GI coffee," he said as he poured out some thick, dark liquid and tossed it away.

Jan laughed loudly. "I've heard a lot about military coffee. Was it *really* that bad?"

He grinned. "Yeah, sometimes it looked and smelled just like what I poured out, and that was when it was first brewed."

She smiled. "Come on, Ryan, let's get back and see what Curt can do with this electricity maker."

They turned across to the beach, continued to the Hump and stopped. "How about you taking the gear door around, and I'll bring the generator. It's heavy, so the tool kit will have to go separately," Bruce said.

"Maybe I can carry the tools," Jan offered.

"Nah, they're pretty heavy, too. I'll get them. It'll just take a little time, but you can take the headset."

"You'd better be careful with that weight, you could very easily get a hernia," she cautioned.

"Yeah, I know. I just don't want to drop it into the water. That salt would probably do it in fast!" he responded.

"I'll carry the door across, and you take it easy," she said.

"Jan," he began.

"Yes?" she responded and looked at Bruce expectantly.

"It was so good to hear you laugh today," he said as he put his hand on her shoulder.

She continued to look into his eyes. She finally nodded then reached to squeeze his forearm.

They completed their tasks and went on to the campsite. Curt met them and Bruce noticed an improvement in his appearance from the early morning.

"I believe you feel better than you did earlier," Bruce said.

"Oh, yeah. It must be Jan's cooking. She finished chow and left to help you. Looks like she did a good job there, too."

"You've both been buttering me up so I'll stay on KP," she joked.

"Aah, you *know* we wouldn't do *that!*" Bruce said.

Curt laughed and Jan said, "Uh huh!"

"Hey, our spa just bubbled, so I'll go warm up lunch and clean the canteen cup, Bruce," she added.

"Great, my appetite is flourishing again," he said.

Bruce and Curt began tinkering with the generator and Curt concluded that it was in good working order. There was no apparent damage or deterioration from the last five years laying in the aircraft wreckage. After they finished lunch Curt asked Bruce to peel some insulation from the wires attached to the generator. "Okay, take the gear between your hands and roll it as fast as you can," he said.

When he had the shaft turning steadily, Curt touched two of the wire tips together and a tiny spark was visible.

"We're in business, folks. Now if those batteries will respond to a charge, we'll be talking to someone before we know it," Curt said and smiled.

"Let's see if adding water to them has helped any so far," Bruce said and went to touch the batteries' terminals with pliers. There was no indication of life in either of them. "Well, they're still dead, but maybe the generator will do some resurrecting," he said, hopefully.

"I've seen it many times," Curt said.

Day Twenty-three

"Folks, I'm not Dutch, but there's a need for a windmill here, so what do you say we get started?" Curt said after breakfast.

"Sounds good to me and I'm not Dutch either. Where do we start after picking these up?" Bruce asked as he held up a gear door.

"Don't think I'm trying to be bossy or a know-it-all, but you'll have to do the work. I'll show you what I'd do, then we can go from there," Curt said and outlined on the door how they should be cut to produce two propeller blades of equal length.

"No problem with the bossing part. I sure need someone to show me all of this stuff," Bruce replied and picked up the shears to begin snipping at the metal.

"Bruce, let me get those gloves you gave me before this goes any further. You'll have blisters on your fingers as big as eggs very quickly," Jan said and went to her hammock.

"All right, thanks. I'm glad someone here has gray matter, I'd be in terrible shape if I had to think for myself," Bruce quipped.

As the work progressed, Bruce asked Curt about its final stages. He explained that once the doors had been reduced to propeller-shaped strips, they could remove bushings on the generator shaft holding the gear that fit onto the engine. The eight propeller blades would replace the gear, and the bushings would be set back in place to hold them. They would have to erect a tripod of bamboo to mount the windmill as high as possible above the ground. The only remaining thing was connecting the wiring from the generator to the batteries.

Bruce completed the cutout work by late morning and stopped for a smoke break. By then Jan had finished preparing their lunch. They sat down to eat and discuss the project further.

"You know, if I don't get the hole in those props exactly in the middle, we're going to have an out-of-balance wobbler," Bruce said, grinning.

"Ryan, speaking of gray matter, take a piece of cord and cut it the length of the metal. Double it, lay it back down, and there you have the exact center," Jan offered.

They all laughed. "By golly, for a Texas girl, you're a smart cookie. I was mentally condemning our lack of a measuring device," he said.

"I think now that the props are done, the tripod is the next step. We can always mount the blades quickly, but they could get bent out of shape if we put them on the generator and let it lay around. If they're bent very much, we will have that wobbler you mentioned for sure, Bruce," Curt said.

"Okay, we don't want to repeat any of these steps if we can help it. I'll get the largest bamboo poles I can find. That generator weighs a lot, and shouldn't be allowed to fall once it's up," Bruce offered.

"Yeah, that might wreck the project quickly," Curt said.

When twilight arrived, Bruce had completed the tripod, connected it to the generator and mounted the blades. He was unable to raise the legs to their full extent by himself. Jan held one of its legs stationary while he moved the other two inward. It was in place, finally.

Day Twenty-four

When Bruce awoke, daylight had fully arrived and rays of the sun were streaking into the shelter. From his hammock, he glanced at Curt and over to Jan's hammock. Both were sleeping soundly. Then he looked to the windmill and was shocked to see the blades revolving slowly in a gentle breeze. Why in hell am I surprised, he thought, that's what we built it for, to turn over and generate electric current.

Shortly Bruce had a fire going and was mixing the final helpings of the coffee into three makeshift cups. After his was heated, he sat back and lit a cigarette to go with it. "Ryan, you're back at the old wake up ritual again," Jan said quietly and smiled.

He grinned. "Yeah, at it again, but today is the last of the Mohegan's. Tomorrow you'll be able to sleep late unless you go back to smoking," he countered.

She shook her head. "No, I think not," she said and took the bamboo cane holding her cup. "I'll tarry over this one, though."

Curt joined them shortly. "Well, guess I'm tail-end Charlie this morning. The mud does smell good."

"It looks like coconut meat and water for breakfast this morning," Jan said. "What we really need is a fridge to keep some of this food."

"Well, maybe next trip we'll figure out a way to build one, or just have one flown in," Curt said and they laughed.

"At least, the windmill works. You two did a great job," Jan said, looking toward it.

"And we had some fine help along the way, too," Bruce said.

"I'll say, the KP corps was the most important part of the whole operation," Curt added and Jan smiled.

"What do you say we start with the circuitry, Bruce? There's a good wind. Might as well do a test flight, and if she charges, then we'll have a live battery and a working radio soon," Curt said.

"Okay, suits me. Harry had half a roll of friction tape in the toolbox, and that should be enough to cover all of the splices if we conserve it as we go along," he replied.

"Yeah, we should do that so they're all covered, and since the sailcloth is larger than the coverlets, I think we should cut off a small strip of that and cover the generator. It may not hurt it to get a little wet, but we don't want rust to start before she does her thing."

"While you two do that, I'm going fishing. I have a feeling they'll be biting today, and fish sounds far more appealing than another round of crab meat," Jan said and left for the beach.

Bruce cut a strip from the sail, tied cords to both ends and tossed one end over the generator. Then he tied the cords to the bamboo scaffolding and a cover for the generator was complete. He and Curt started through the hookup for the electrical system, beginning with the battery and working toward a final connection two feet from the generator. Bruce did the splices and taping while Curt looked on. He connected one of the wires coming from the generator and applied tape. "Well, here's the final one. Do you think this thing will burn me when I hook the last one together?" he asked.

"Nah, I'll go over and stop the blades from turning until you complete the splice," Curt replied. "You've got it now. Just twist it together and tape it," Curt said and waited a moment. "Okay, I'm releasing the blades, so the juice should flow."

Curt came back to the battery and placed a screwdriver over the terminal posts. Immediately, there was a sharp crack of electric current. "Bruce, ol' buddy, we're now in the current-making business," he said.

"Hey, that's great! Wonder how long it'll take before we know whether the battery will hold a charge?" Bruce asked.

"Well, the generator is turning much slower here than when it's on an engine, but I'd guess by dark today, with any kind of wind at all, we should be able to tell," Curt replied.

"Good. I hope the wind doesn't decide to shift from the southwest. The gen is stationary and can't follow it." Bruce said.

"You're right, but I've noticed it blows from that direction almost all of the time. I think it'll be adequate," Curt said.

In the distance there came a familiar drone of aircraft engine noise. Bruce picked up signal mirrors and ran toward the beach. The Connie was visible for only moments as it passed behind scattered clouds to the north. He jiggled the mirrors back and forth. The sun's angle gave no glimmer at all and the engine noise faded without any change in tone. Looking toward the northwest first, he saw a large rain shower that appeared to be moving into the area. Then he saw Jan at her favorite fishing spot and walked toward her.

"My luck with the mirrors was nil. How's the fishing fortunes?"

"Not very good. I caught two minnows earlier and threw them back, then hooked a nice one but the rascal got off my hook before I could land it," she replied.

"Well, rats! The regular for dinner again, but I reckon that beats nothing any day of the week, huh?" he jested.

Jan smiled. "Yes, it definitely could be worse," she said as a loud rumble of thunder grumbled close by. "Sounds like we'd better run for the shelter or we'll be wet soon," she added.

They walked hurriedly across the beach toward camp just as a few drops of rain began to fall. "We got the generator system hooked up, and it seems to be working well, but we'll have to wait and see whether the battery holds a charge. Curt thinks there will probably be an indication by nightfall," Bruce said.

"That's great! Let's keep our fingers crossed and maybe say a little prayer, too. It would be nice just to hear a voice from the outside world again," she replied.

A moment after they reached the shelter rain arrived, light at first, then a heavy downpour began with winking lightning and a heavy thunder. Winds were gusty and variable in direction, and the generator blades turned sporadically. After the shower passed, the wind became light and northerly, and the blades were completely still at first, but finally began turning slowly in reverse. As the breeze gradually shifted back to the southwest, the blades resumed a rapid revolution in the right direction.

The survivors stayed in the shelter until the rain stopped, and then each resumed light activity outside. "Jan, tell you what, since you made such a gallant effort to fish, I'll round up some crab for supper," Bruce said.

"Now, that's big of you, Ryan. You catch 'em, and I'll cook 'em," she replied.

"You nice folks do that, and ol' crip will eat," Curt said and laughed softly.

While Bruce went around gathering crabs, Jan picked breadfruit and bamboo shoots, then she went for a cup of sea water to heat and season their food once it was cooked. After the items were in the spa, the trio gathered at the firesite to wait. "You know," Jan began, "we have been living together here almost a month, but actually we're all still strangers. Why don't we tell our life's story, or most of it anyway," she suggested.

"Okay, it'll help pass the time. You first," Bruce said.

"Oh, no! One of you go first, I need to think about mine some more," she replied.

"Mine is too dull to even pass time," Curt joked.

"And mine's too boring to tell. Save the worst for last. Anyway, it's ladies first," Bruce added.

"Looks like I've talked myself into a corner. One day I'll learn to keep my trap shut, maybe! But first, I was born twenty-three years ago in Angleton, south of Houston. My parents operate an accounting firm there. That's where I grew up, went to high school and all the other regular stuff. I was a part-time cheerleader and a color bearer for the band. Social studies and home ec were my best subjects. After high school I went to Houston Junior College in '45 to be either a teacher or home economist.

"By the second year I'd decided on home ec and was pursuing that diligently in '47 when along came Benjamin Clinner on the GI Bill. We started dating. Ben had gone into the Army in '42. He was four years older than I. He was nice and seemed to have been everywhere and done everything. The older man syndrome, I guess.

"One thing led to another and he convinced me that we should get married. After I graduated from junior college we had the traditional church wedding and settled down into married life. I didn't continue on in school, but he stayed at the University of Houston to graduate the next year. I took a part-time job to occupy myself and earn extra money, too.

"We continued for a few months. and then difficulty set in for me. Ben was possessive all along, I knew, but then his jealousy began to emerge, mainly concerning my job as receptionist in a man's clothier. I couldn't even visit my family unless he was there. I have two younger sisters, and we're probably closer than most girls are. They couldn't comprehend such an attitude, then my parents began to wonder what his problem was about the same time as I did. To make a long story short, we separated, and problems increased several fold. He couldn't accept possessiveness and jealousy as the reasons why I left him. He repeatedly said there must be someone else. There wasn't!

"Ben kept coming to my parents' home—really just making a nuisance of himself, following me, calling at odd hours, and parking out front of the house to see when I came and left. In early '49 I was back in school again, but he kept on with the spying bit, and I wasn't making progress with my studies. Then I saw an ad in the paper for a job as a stewardess. Am-Mex hired me, so I told Ben if he could afford to fly almost every day, then he could keep up his vigil.

"I've seen him a couple of times since our divorce, and there was little change in him the best I could tell. He's a nice guy basically, never was violent or anything like that. Just too covetous and old before his time. He wouldn't even consider having children.

"That's about it. A typical girl-next-door thing. I've enjoyed my work with the airline, and as soon as we get off Shoe Island, I'll go back into the wild blue."

"You left out the beauty contests part. Since you look so much like Gail Russell there must have been a bunch of loving cups and first place ribbons given out," Bruce said.

She laughed. "Ryan, I've been told that I look like Gail Russell before and I'm flattered. She's a very pretty woman. But up until my marriage I resembled a beanstalk. In high school the most I weighed was a hundred pounds, and the boys all thought I was one of *them* judging from my straight lines. No, nothing was left out," she concluded and smiled.

"How about it? Anymore Bens, Sams, or Johns pursuing you and talking matrimony?" Bruce jested.

"No, none of those either," she began and laughed. "Most of the guys with the airline were in military service before signing on, and apparently 1946 was the year that everybody got married when they were released from active duty. Guess I'll have to wait for some of the younger ones to get through college."

"Aah, I don't think you're really serious about getting marred again. When you are, you won't have any trouble, I'm sure," Curt said.

"I really haven't thought about it much. I've waited to see how the job turned out. I love flying and enjoy what I do, so why tie myself down until I'm sure?" she replied.

"Well, how about the last flight? Did it change your mind about flying any?" Bruce chuckled.

She smiled and waited for a moment to speak. "No, not really. Everyone that flies thinks about crashes sometimes, but I suppose we all figure it won't happen to us. It's always someone else, you know. The fatal or serious ones, that is."

"According to my friends in the business, that's the *only* way to look at it. Otherwise, it'll drive you batty to sweat it all of the time," Curt said.

"Well, enough of that stuff. I'll get the food from the spa, and Bruce, will you get a fire started to heat some water? A little salt in our diet helps the blands, don't you think?" Jan continued.

"Yeah, it sure does, and I'm gonna get with it right now, ma'am!" Bruce responded.

Chapter Eleven

Day Twenty-five

Daylight came at a snail's pace for Bruce. He longed for a cup of coffee. He had awakened early and lay quietly listening to Curt snore lightly inside the shelter. Then he heard Jan turning in her hammock on the opposite side. His cigarette tasted dry and weedy, but he took several long pulls on it and crushed it out in the sand under his hammock. Jan. By golly, that girl has had a round of life already. I'm surprised she married so young, and that guy must have been a real nut. But she's one pretty woman, and if she were mine, maybe I'd be jealous too. There are extremes in everything, he thought to himself.

Bruce quietly left camp for the beach at first light and he walked down to the waterline. Small waves were breaking and he noted increased wind at his back. "I'll be danged," he thought aloud, "we never did check the battery last night to see if it was charged. When the others get up, I'll do that." He watched the methodical action of the sea.

As the water continued its motion, Bruce's mind changed to the A-26. Maybe I should go back there and get those guys out. I could wrap the remains in a chute and bind that up with the risers. It just seems disrespectful to leave them as they are. I'll do that today after Jan and Curt are awake. He lit another cigarette and took occasional, small puffs while he looked out to sea. A few scattered clouds had formed in the distance, otherwise the sun rose in a clear, azure sky.

"It's beautiful and peaceful out there this morning, isn't it?" Jan said and Bruce turned in surprise.

"Yeah, it sure is. A little too peaceful, though," he replied and laughed softly.

"How long have you been up?" she asked.

"Oh, since first light. An hour I guess. It gets around to coffee time and up I get," he laughed.

"Boy, a hot cup would be great, wouldn't it?" she said.

"Yeah, but we'll be off this paradise soon once we get the radio working. Then we can drink long cups of coffee every day."

They both smiled and turned to look longingly at the north horizon. "Jan, I was thinking that I'd go back and get those men's remains out of the plane and wrap them in a chute. Somehow, it just doesn't seem right to leave them as they are. What do you think?"

"Well, it's a nice gesture, but where will you put them? The plane is a better tomb than out in the open. Maybe bundle them up and just leave them in the aircraft. I don't know what's best."

"Yeah, that's a good idea. One chute will be enough for all three. But first, I'm going to check the battery and see if it's holding a charge. Is Curt awake yet?"

"Yeah, I saw him going to the john a little while after I got up."

Bruce went to the battery and removed one wire from the circuit hookup. He placed a screwdriver across the terminal posts and moved it back and forth. There was no response at all. Disappointment stabbed at him. Damn, I was sure we'd have a little life in that thing, he thought. Well, I'll get the other one and try it for a while. Maybe it'll do the job. He brought the second battery and completed the connections, then looked to the blades. They were turning over in a light wind. "Okay, baby, do your thing," he said, hopefully.

While they sat having a breakfast of coconut milk and meat, Bruce told the others there was no current stored in the first battery.

"It might have been shot to begin with," Curt began. "Sometimes aircraft batteries just go out all at once. They might have left a switch on at the time of the crash that drained it."

"Well, we have another and it's going to work. I can tell," Jan offered.

Bruce laughed softly.

"Why are you laughing? Oh, I know, my fish stories," she said.

They all laughed. "She's hooked up, and by noon today it should show some life if it's going to," Bruce explained.

After breakfast Bruce told Curt of his plans regarding the crewmen. "I think that's a great idea. I'm like you, it doesn't seem quite right to just leave them as they are," he replied.

"Well, folks, I'm off to the broken bird. I'll check again, but I think there's nothing left in it that we can use," Bruce said.

"I don't want to see the operation while you're doing it, but as soon as I get some lunch in the oven, I'll come down too. I want to get some nylon from one of the chutes and practice my sewing," Jan said.

"And while you two do that, I'll check back over our electrical system to be sure we don't have any loose connections. I can't see why it wouldn't work, so it's probably because the battery is the weak link," Curt added.

They all started at their tasks without further comments. Bruce went around the Hump and down the beach to the bomber site. He decided to wrap the remains and place them inside the cockpit. It will be easier to remove them from there if help ever arrives from the outside world, he thought. Then his mind went back to the battery. Damn, that thing has to work! It's our only chance of getting out of here. But even if it does charge, will it produce enough current to operate the radio?

First, Bruce took Ken's chute and cut away the heavy covering with the survival knife. Next he slit three strips of the nylon and began. The lines were used to bundle Ken and Steven, then he went to the tail and carried Harry to the cockpit. He placed the three bundles just behind the seats, looked over the interior again and closed the canopy back securely. Remembering that he hadn't closed the hatch door on the rear compartment, he went back and drew out Harry's chest pack chute. This will be enough for Jan to work on, he thought, then closed the small door and went around to the left wing and sat down by the engine to smoke.

Bruce leaned back, pulled on his cigarette and wiped a trickle of sweat on his forehead. Well, I guess that's no noble deed, but at least I feel I've done something for the three of them. He closed his eyes and continued smoking. Then he heard Jan before she spoke.

"All right, Ryan, on your feet. Enough of that goofing off."

"Okay, *Sergeant* Adams! I'm getting there," he replied and laughed as he turned to look at the pretty girl.

"Finished already?"

"Yeah, it didn't take very long. I took your suggestion and put them all in the cockpit. I looked over the interior again. I think we have everything worthwhile. No more supplies left."

Jan came and sat down next to him. "Bruce, I don't mean to burden you with the past, but sometimes around Curt I start shivering inside. I know he deeply regrets what happened, although he's never said anything else about it. It's on his face and in his voice when he speaks to me. Oftentimes, I just have to get up and leave until the feeling passes."

"Yeah, I can only imagine how you must feel," he said as he reached to take her hand. "Just hang on a little longer, we'll get off this dune and be able to put a lot of things behind us."'

Her face turned away and Bruce knew she was crying. He put his arms around her, held her close and stroked her back. Then she began to relax and he withdrew. "Come on, let's get over to the beach, and we'll stroll along. Just take the long way home."

She nodded and stepped off rapidly. "Jan, take it easy. It'll pass. Remember, some of those cow piles need rewashing and the nose blown again sometimes."

She laughed heartily.

They ambled along the beach making small talk about Houston, and Jan took the cigarette that Bruce offered. After a few puffs she flipped it into the water. "Ryan, those cigs are worse than the rabbit tobacco we used to smoke as kids. How do you stand them?"

"I don't know. They're bad all right and just barely beat having none at all. Maybe I should try and quit."

"It would be easy for me if I smoked those things."

Bruce laughed.

After they passed the Hump and neared camp, Curt greeted them. "Good news, folks! We are getting a charge in the battery this time," he called.

"Hey, that's great!" Bruce exclaimed.

"Yes, it certainly is. Have you just checked it?" Jan asked.

"Yeah, I couldn't stand the waiting, so I went over and the ol' screwdriver definitely caused a perk when I placed it over the terminals. Not much of one, but a spark at least!"

"How long do you think it'll take for enough power to build up to operate the radio?" Bruce asked.

"It's hard to say. I'd guess a couple of days, if we get those southwest winds. Less if they should increase or blow at night, which isn't very often. But the radios have a power booster feature built in. A little juice and the output is full strength."

"That's great! I guess we play a waiting game for a while and give it a whirl later to check the progress," Bruce said.

"Is anyone interested in having our next meal now, or shall we postpone it until later?" Jan asked.

"Let's eat now. while it's fresh," Bruce suggested.

"Okay, I'll go upstairs and bring it down. Then one of you can tell us your life's story," she said.

As she left for the spa, Bruce said, "My story is so dull, why don't you go first, Curt? I just have so little to tell."

"Bruce, if yours is any more uninteresting than mine, I don't see how you've made it this long," he replied and grinned.

"Tell you what, I have a few coins in my pocket. Let's flip for last, call it," Bruce said as he tossed a quarter up.

"Heads."

"You win. I'll go first."

Jan returned shortly with the food and they began their meal. After they finished Curt said, "Mr. Ryan will now give us details and highlights of his life in Texas and other parts unknown."

Jan giggled and looked at Bruce.

"Let me double check my coin first, it probably has two heads. Jan, I flipped him for last place—he won," Bruce said and they all laughed. "Well, I was born and raised in Humble. That's just north of Houston. I'll be twenty-four on May first. I have two younger brothers and my parents still live in Humble. My dad works in the oil field supply business. In high school I played football and baseball although not very well, but both were a lot of fun. In late '44 after I'd registered for the draft, I decided to enlist in the Air Corps for the duration plus six months rather than wait and be drafted into the ground forces.

"After basic training at San Antonio, I was assigned to a casual pool, until they could decide what to do with me. Mainly, I pulled KP or guard duty and picked up cigarette butts. It was there that I picked up my one-millionth butt. We were out one day pursuing the second and some 'hot shot' pilot had a P-47 Thunderbolt up wringing it out, and I decided then I wanted to be a pilot. So, I applied and darned if they didn't accept me. I moved from the San Antonio Army Air Base to Kelly Field and started at the bottom of the totem pole again. But my pay increased from a private's to a staff sergeant's and I thought, as a cadet, I was making progress.

"After I got into primary training, they told my group one day that our class had been canceled. That was it! The war in Europe was over and I guess somebody figured the Pacific fighting would end shortly too. Then they told us we could apply for assignment in anything else. Someone suggested a control tower job, and I asked for that. Away I went to the tower for on-the-job training. In October of '45, several of us were called in by the CO and asked to reenlist. *I said* no thank you, and *they said* pack your bags and go home, boy."

"Then I heard about the CAA needing controllers at the state employment office and went to Hobby Airport to apply. They took me, and again, back to the bottom of the proverbial pole! But after a year in training status I became a journeyman and have stayed there until now. Meantime, I built an apartment over my parents' garage and sort of let the rest of the world rock on by. But a job in Hawaii came open and tickled my fancy. I bid on it and they took me. However, before I got there, well, the Am-Mex thing has me back in a familiar spot again."

They all laughed. "That's it?" Jan asked.

"That's it! I told you, my name should've been Bruce Dull."

"Well, what about a girl? You didn't mention a thing about the romance in your life," she said.

Bruce laughed softly. "There wasn't much! I dated a girl my senior year of high school. We vowed our devotion to each other right up to the time I left for basic. Just after I arrived at Kelly, she sent me a typical Dear John. She had met an 4-Fer in Houston, and—"

"And you're back at the bottom of that pole again," Jan quipped.

"Yep, right back in my familiar spot. There was a WAC at Kelly. Boy, she was a pretty thing, exactly five feet tall and about a hundred pounds soaking wet. She was two years older than me and had a lot of GI Bill training coming to her. So, she got out of the Army to attend college and planned to go back in as an officer. We were pretty serious for a while, but she had her goals and I'd had all of the military that I wanted. She was from Decatur, Alabama, and in December '48 she came through Houston, flying home for the holidays. She was a first looey in the Air Force and was assigned to March Air Force Base, California. Naturally, she told me after we met at the airport that she was engaged to some shavetail out there."

Jan giggled long and merrily. "Bruce, that totem pole has been with you a long time, hasn't it?"

Curt laughed. "Hang in there, buddy, you've got a lot of time left, and totem poles have a way of disappearing."

"Yeah, I guess so. My mom tells me I'm too young to marry anyway. You know how mamas are, still a kid in her eyes."

The survivors whiled away the day's remaining light with small talk and snacked on coconut meat, then retired.

Chapter Twelve

Day Twenty-six

Just before daylight there was a loud crash of thunder and vivid flashes of lightning preceding a rush of strong wind and heavy rain. Jan and Bruce ran from their hammocks to the shelter before getting wet. The rain continued to pour, and shortly leaks started and made puddles inside the shelter. The occupants kept shifting around to stay dry until well after daybreak.

"Well, folks, it's a gully washer all right, but at least the wind is a good one from the right direction. The electrons are flowing into the battery," Curt said finally.

"They can't get there soon enough for me," Bruce began, "and by day's end we should see a good charge built up. If this lasts all day, maybe tomorrow we can test the radio gear."

"Speaking of radio gear, Bruce, there's one thing we haven't done. We've got to get the antenna anchored in one of these palm trees as high as possible," Curt said.

"Yeah, you're right. I'd forgotten about that. When the rain stops I'll get it up there somewhere."

Jan laughed softly.

"What?" Bruce asked.

"Well, there are no totem poles here, and this time you'll be climbing up—not going down."

Bruce grinned. "Yeah, I guess so. I think I'll take the antenna and tie it as high as I can, then secure the receiver cable back down the tree some. That should give us about twenty-five feet of height. I don't think we'll be able to get up much higher. The Hump is taller, but there isn't enough wire to reach that far. What do you think, Curt?"

"Sounds good to me, and I think it will be sufficient height to reach out twenty miles or so, with everything at sea level," he said.

Rain continued for most of the morning, and nearing noon a glaring sun broke through heavy clouds when it stopped. Jan gathered some coconuts for a breakfast snack, and Bruce began assembling material before starting to climb a palm tree. After eating, he made the climb and installed the antenna equipment as he had planned. Then he came down and stretched a lead wire from the shelter to another wire dangling on the antenna base. He completed the splicing quickly.

"While you were up there," Curt said, "I did another check, we're definitely getting more of a charge in the battery. It cracked pretty good when I applied the screwdriver."

"Okay! Man, that's what we need, more power," Bruce replied.

"I'm going fishing. Crab for supper doesn't seem appetizing," Jan said and left for the beach.

"Bruce, I hate to ask, but I wonder if you'd give me an assist up the hill. It's been a few days since I've been in the spa and I probably need it," Curt said.

"You bet, anytime you're ready."

"How about right now?"

"You've got it. Should be cooler by now. I heard it spewing half an hour ago."

They made their way up the lava chute with little difficulty, and Curt went into the water. Bruce spent the time standing on the leaning palm tree scanning over the island and horizon. Cloud cover was diminishing and a strong breeze continued from the southwest. He could see Jan on the beach, but there was nothing else of interest so he went down to the spa.

"Man, that water sure does make the ol' body feel better. I think it must have some therapeutic value. I'd like to take it with me when we go home," Curt said.

"Yeah, it does make a difference in your feelings. Maybe we should get you in it more often. Does it do anything for the numbness?"

"Nah, not that I can tell, and it's such a tussle to get up here, I really hate to ask so much."

"No sweat on that, Curt, I'll help you anytime. All we can do now is wait on the battery charge anyway. Maybe more baths will help blood circulation if nothing else."

As they started descending Jan called out, "Are you two coming down now?"

"Yeah, should be just another minute or two," Bruce replied.

"Okay, I made a haul on fishing today. Guess the weather change had them hopping. Should be a great dinner," she said.

"That sounds outstanding to me. The crab is beginning to talk back somewhat," Curt replied.

When they reached the sandy floor, she had five large fish and the knife ready to climb to the spa for cleaning and cooking. "Hey, a couple of those beauties are large enough to mount," Bruce said.

"Well, as soon as they're done, I'm going to mount some large chunks of them on my tongue," Jan replied.

At twilight, Jan returned with the fish, breadfruit, and bamboo shoots for their meal. They ate leisurely and darkness came before all of them had finished. Bruce kindled the fire and each took a turn at making small talk. When that began to drag, Jan reminded Curt it was his turn to tell his life's story to them.

"Both of you have surpassed my experiences so much, I hate to even begin telling such a drab story," he said and Bruce and Jan both realized suddenly that his speech was less slurred now than it had been for the last week or so.

"Excuse my interruption, but Curt your speech is better than it's been in a while. I just noticed it," Bruce said.

"I started to say the same thing. Do you suppose it's those, aah, what are they, APC?" Jan said.

"Beats me, I hadn't noticed any change except some words are easier for me to say now. Who knows?" Curt began. "Anyway, on with the Myrick yarn, and I'll have you both bored out of your skulls before I've finished high school, but here goes.

"I was born near Enid, Oklahoma in 1921 and grew up on a ranch at Breckinridge. The small school that I attended didn't have any organized sports. We played a little sandlot baseball and that was it. I was bussed to high school in Enid my last two years because of some reorganizing. In '38 when I finished there wasn't much of anything going on, and I couldn't go to college because the Depression wasn't over yet.

"My parents own a three hundred-acre ranch, and I have two younger brothers and sisters. They raise cattle and a few horses.

That just wasn't my thing. So, I went into Enid and started working at a garage, a flunky, really. By 1940 I'd begun to pick up a little on auto repairs, then FDR sent me a greeting to report for the draft, but I went to Oklahoma City and enlisted in the Navy. All that walking the Army does never did appeal to me very much.

"After boot camp at Great Lakes, Illinois, they sent me to Pensacola and said I was going to be an aircraft mechanic. Of course, I was in schools over the next year or so. Then I went back to Enid for ten days leave. A girl that I dated before the war was still there, and we decided to get married. She followed me around to various places at her own expense. Her parents were pretty well off. Then I drew a carrier assignment and that ended our togetherness for a while. In '43 we took some heavy damage and went back to Mare Island, California for extensive repairs. She met me there."

Curt chuckled and paused for a moment. "It's funny, after two days everything was rocking along about normal. We had supper and sat down in the living room of our two-room apartment. She reached over and took my hand, then looked at me with a little grin on her face. She said, 'Rick,' at first it was *Myrick*, then later just Rick. 'I'm going back to Oklahoma tomorrow. I like you very much, but I'm not in love with you, as it should be in marriage. How do you feel?'

"I told her I felt the same. We had let the war influence us into making a very big mistake. She's a fine woman, and I was attracted to her good looks and strong personality.

"The next morning I went off to duty and she went to the train station. We parted the best of friends and have written to each other occasionally since. I saw her briefly in '46 when I went home for a visit. She's now a fashion writer for ladies' publications. You might have seen her picture or read some of her articles. Ingrid Heilbron, a typical blonde, blue-eyed Kraut. I lost track of her after I decided to remain in Hawaii.

"One of the lieutenants that I served with flew my plane until the A-bomb was dropped, then we were sent back to Pearl and waited until the surrender was official. While there, the lieutenant talked to me about working for him. His family built Wall Street, I think, and they had things geared up for a freight hauling airline as soon as the war ended. It sounded like a good deal to me, so I took my discharge and signed on with him. They bought some R5Ds and R6Ds—DC-4s and 6s—from the government and we were in business by October '45. Most of the cargo was items to get the Japanese back on their feet, and all I had to do was make sure the birds held together and flew.

"Our base of operations remained in Honolulu, and the lieutenant was a dabbler in real estate, so he got me involved with it. Fortunately for me, we made some right choices, and several of our holdings worked out well. I went back to Oklahoma to see my parents. Both aren't as well as they once were. On the way back to the ol' grind, strange things happened with Am-Mex."

They all laughed. "Are you still working on aircraft for your company?" Jan asked after a moment.

"Nah, not really. I'm a straw boss now and just sort of see to it that the birds are maintained."

"That's not Click Airline is it?" Bruce asked.

"That's us."

"I'll be darned. I've worked some of your birds in and out of Houston. That's a big outfit from what I've heard."

"Yeah, we've grown steadily. I forget how many planes there are, but we operate in the States and worldwide. In fact, we've made more flights to Europe than anywhere else since the war. We have ports in New York, South Carolina, Miami and two on the West Coast plus the one in Honolulu."

"And you've never married again?" Jan ventured.

"No, I guess I'm a confirmed bachelor. Lieutenant—uh, Ted McDonough, I call him lieutenant, he calls me chief—went back home and married after the war. His wife has at least a thousand girlfriends, and they all want to visit Hawaii. She is an extraordinary matchmaker and has fixed me up with half of them. But somehow the right one just hasn't come along yet."

"How about it, still carrying the torch for Ingrid?" Jan asked.

"Nah, I don't think so. As I said, she's a fine woman and we are good friends, or were. But we sort of struck out in the romance department. I'm just glad there were no children as a result of our mistake. She said the same thing."

"Oh, well, you're still young. Miss Right will come along one of these days when you least expect it," Bruce offered.

"Yeah, could be. But first I have to get back somewhere for a general overhaul on my ignition system. You know, get to hitting on all eight cylinders again."

"Aah, you'll be able to do that in no time. You're in good health and therapy will get you back in shape. When the battery heats up we'll be off this dune in a hurry," Bruce replied.

"An innerspring mattress would be the best therapy I could get right now," Jan said and they all laughed.

"Well, folks, ol' Curt has bored you enough. I'm gonna sack out and dream of radio transmissions and seaplanes landing in our front yard for the rest of the night."

Day Twenty-seven

Bruce lay quietly smoking and listening to familiar sounds in the pale morning light. Curt snored intermittently. Jan coughed and turned in her hammock. Birds chattered above them. Then came the unmistakable drone of a B-29's engines in the distance. Bruce scrambled up and ran to the beach with a signal mirror. Damn! he thought as the aircraft made a quick bank to the northwest. That bird can't be more than twelve miles north and at ten grand. Oh, well, there's no sun to reflect on the mirror anyway, but I could have started the signal fire or shot a flare. Why didn't I think of that?

Jan was standing nearby when he turned around. "That one was much closer than the others, wasn't it?" she said.

"Yeah, I'd guess twelve miles and about ten thousand feet. It was a B-29, and you know the Air Corps, I mean Force. Those rascals were probably tooling around and got off course. Too bad they didn't tool on down this way a little more."

"Well, maybe next time," she said wearily.

They returned to camp and Bruce began stoking the fire out of habit, then took out a cigarette.

"You really miss that mud in the morning, don't you, Ryan?" Jan said and smiled.

"Yeah, I do, and I was thinking, hurry up and get a shot of coconut cocktail," he replied.

Curt joined them then. "That plane was closer and lower than most, wasn't it?"

"Yeah, it was a B-29 Superfortress at about twelve miles and ten thousand feet," Bruce said.

"Well, another day or so and we'll be able to call them into our lagoon. I just have a gut feeling, for whatever that's worth," Curt chuckled.

After opening coconuts and drinking the milk, they began munching on the meat in silence. Shortly, Jan rose, gathered material and began snipping at parachute fabric with the scissors from Harry's sewing kit. Bruce looked at the windmill and saw that it was turning. "I'm gonna check the battery's charge, then go down with your gear and land a big one this morning. Okay, Sergeant Adams?"

"Captain Ryan, be my guest. Good luck," Jan replied and smiled.

"I'll take an APC and get off my crutch again," Curt said, then added, "Bruce, let me know about the battery, please."

"You bet!"

He went over to the battery with a screwdriver, then turned back as Curt approached. "I think we're making progress. There is definitely more power in the battery today. Like you said at the start, it's just a slow process," Bruce said.

"That's good news for sure. I thought it would take a while. The props are turning so much slower, but we'll get there yet."

Bruce left for the beach and began fishing. He caught several small fish and tossed them back into the water. As his crab meat bait started to diminish, he had lost patience and loaded the hook with all of the remaining scraps. When the line settled into the water, the small pole almost left his hand with a strong pull from below. He wrestled with the pole until it became difficult to hold, then stepped into the water for slack and to grasp the line. He walked back toward the beach and hauled in a large fish.

"Well I'll be darned. You're a lucky rascal after all, Ryan. That fish has to weigh six to eight pounds. What did you use for bait?" Jan said as she walked up to him.

"Just regular ol' crab meat. I loaded the hook pretty heavily though. Really, I got tired of fooling with them and put all I had on the hook, planning to quit when the minnows got that," he replied and grinned.

"Why don't we try to roast this one. The boiling is getting old for me. How about you?" she said.

"Yeah, that's a good idea. I'll clean it and rig a stake over the fire so it can be turned frequently. The heat and smoke should do the rest. Then, tonight, we feast!"

"Mmmm, I can hardly wait! With a little salt water basting, that sounds like great eating," she replied.

"How's the sewing progressing?"

"Slowly. I have to sew a stitch, then go to the john for fitting and come back for more hemming," she said and giggled.

"Oh, you're making *those*?"

"Yeah," she said and smiled, "and transferring the elastic is a tougher job than I thought it would be. But a case of have to."

"Yeah, I know what you mean, mine are taking a beating too. So far, no holes, just threadbare."

They went back to camp and Bruce prepared to go to the spa and clean their fish. Curt appeared to be sleeping and they didn't disturb him.

"Tell you what, Ryan, since you did the catching and plan to build our cookery, I'll take this minnow to the spa and clean it. I have to clean me too, so two birds, you know."

"Hey, you're all right, if I do say so myself. Wait, I'll even run the knife down for you. Let's see, it should be here somewhere."

"Bruce, if I take the knife, how will you cut bamboo for the cooking poles?"

"By gum, and smart too! I hadn't thought of that, but you *can* take the small knife from the bomber. It'll clean that critter," he replied and they laughed.

Both went on with their tasks, and shortly after noon the fish was mounted over a small fire that Bruce rekindled. Curt had joined them earlier and shared their delight in anticipation of a different meal. For the remainder of the afternoon the survivors passed time with small talk and various tasks they conjured up. As twilight began, Jan probed the fish with a bamboo splinter and determined that it was cooked thoroughly. She added their usual staple items and they lingered long in the enjoyment of the meal.

Chapter Thirteen

Day Twenty-eight

A definite change in weather had occurred. Strong, gusty winds raked the small island from the southwest, while clouds thickened and raced by above. As the day wore on, there was an occasional sprinkle and heavy rains swept by in all directions. "It looks like we're in for lousy weather sooner or later," Curt said over breakfast as the three sat in their shelter.

"Yeah, it seems like I can smell rain. I guess it's because of the mist we've had all morning. I've put some more firewood inside just in case," Bruce said.

"Well, whatever it's going to do, it sure has rotated the windmill. Earlier, those blades looked like an aircraft propeller. That should help the battery charge," Jan added.

For the rest of the day conditions remained the same. As darkness fell, periods of heavy rain lashed at the tiny lava oasis along with a raging, tossing sea.

During the night the trio was forced to keep moving around inside the shelter to avoid dripping water, and occasionally gusty winds sprayed each of them with cold wetness. All of them used their vinyl to cover the radio and electrical equipment.

Day Twenty-nine

Daylight arrived, the rain tapered off, then finally stopped. But strong winds continued to lash at the island and a roaring sea sent crashing waves to batter its shoreline. The windmill continued to rotate at a high RPM rate, and Bruce began checking the wiring system to ensure that winds and moisture had not caused any of the splices to separate. "I think we should fire up the radio this morning and see what it'll do," he said.

"While we have this wind and a steady flow of current to the battery, it might not be a bad idea," Curt replied.

"Why don't you wait until around noon when the Connie is in our area?" Jan said.

"This is Friday, so yeah you're right, I should. We won't have enough power to reach Hawaii, and if we don't have any luck today we can try again tomorrow for the return flight," Bruce laughed.

Curt turned to the radio equipment. "I'll tinker with the receiver first, then I think I'll go ahead and test both units to see if they have enough juice to fire them off. I believe most of the airliners monitor emergency frequencies, and if there's a need, they'll have to reset their transmitter. But that's no problem."

"All of the air traffic facilities monitor them too and switch to whatever the listening frequency is on the aircraft. Most of their transmitters are preset."

"All of the airway stations use 123.5 megacycles for VHF, but I don't know about the overseas people. Do you know what frequencies your company planes monitor, Jan?" Bruce said.

"No, sorry. If I've heard them, I can't remember," she replied.

"Well, friends, the connections are made, and there's a light on in the receiver, but I can't tell about the transmitter. Key the mike, Bruce, and see what we get," Curt said.

Bruce keyed the mike and immediately the receiver began squealing and shrieking. "Hey! Man, we're in business! But let's turn 'em off to conserve power until just after twelve." He checked his watch and saw they would have to wait two hours. Then he looked at the windmill to see whether it was maintaining a good rotation. It was, although not as fast as before.

The minutes dragged slowly by, and Bruce kept checking his watch to ensure the time didn't pass before he tried contacting the aircraft. Finally, noon approached. "Tell you what, folks, everybody listen good, and if anyone hears engine noise, sing out. Otherwise, I'll start transmitting at fifteen after twelve and continue for about five minutes. If they're gonna hear me, that should be long enough. I don't want to drain the battery completely," he said.

There was no engine noise, but at the selected time Curt pulled off one line to the generator so the current came directly from the battery, then motioned to Bruce. He turned the receiver volume off to avoid the squeals and keyed the transmitter. "Mayday! Mayday! Mayday! Am-Mex flight 755 survivors. Does anyone read me?"

Bruce repeated the message intermittently for five minutes by turning the receiver volume down to prevent squeals when he pressed the transmitter key, then turned it back up when he stopped speaking. The mike began making a slight dragging sound, and Bruce clicked the transmitter off, but left the receiver on with its volume up for another five minutes. There still was no response and he snapped it off with a somber grunt. "I guess the wind being from the southwest probably carried the engine noise away from us. But I believe we got out far enough for them to have heard the call. I'm just not sure about the frequency. Maybe I should go back to the A-26 and get a VHF transmitter/receiver. The only thing is a distance bit. It's line of sight, but if no one is monitoring this 3023.5, then it's all in the same boat. I guess we'll keep on trying the high frequency for a few days and just see. What do you two think?"

"I really don't know much about it, so whatever you want to do is okay by me," Jan said.

"It looks to me like the high frequency is our best bet. All of the military planes have it, and I'm sure there are more of those than air carriers," Curt replied.

Day Thirty

Winds had subsided drastically and Bruce looked regularly at the windmill to see whether it was still rotating. He checked his watch often to time a transmission with the arrival of the return flight due north of Shoe Island. "I thought to start transmitting around ten-thirty and continue until thirty-five. Keep your fingers crossed," he said.

"Let me know when it's time, and I'll stand by to shuffle the wiring," Curt began.

"With all of that wind yesterday, I'd think the battery has a good charge and more power. Maybe this will be the one that does the job."

"Yeah, I noticed the windmill turning at a good clip even after I 'hammocked out' last night," Jan said and giggled.

"Maybe you should do the transmitting, Jan. A girl's voice on the horn always gets more attention," Bruce said and grinned.

"No, thank you. I'd be too nervous to speak," she replied.

"Aah, you wouldn't. But it's time, so Curt if you'll do the honors, I'll speak to the public, although I feel like I might as well be signaling with semaphores."

Bruce began transmitting using the same procedures and message as the day before, then repeated them for five minutes. There was no response, but he decided to leave the receiver on for an additional five minutes. After two minutes a high-pitched voice crackled, "Mayday! Navy two four . . . one hundred miles . . . flameout . . ."

The aircraft transmission was broken and badly garbled. Bruce thought of switching the transmitter back on to call the identification he had heard, but he declined for fear of possibly interfering with the pilot's distress call to a control facility.

"At least we know now that should anyone hear our transmission, we'll be able to get a response," Curt said.

"Yes, and it was so nice just to hear a voice from the outside world for a change. I hope that Navy pilot makes it in okay," Jan said.

The morning dragged slowly on and after lunch the despondent trio lounged into the afternoon. Jan decided to take another try at fishing, and Curt opted for a nap when the APC made him drowsy. Bruce tinkered with the wiring system checking for any breaks in the circuit. Then he decided to climb up the palm tree again and inspect the antenna wiring as well. It was all intact.

Jan caught enough fish for their evening meal, then went about preparing them along with the staple items. As twilight faded into darkness, the three of them lingered over their food but each showed little interest in small talk. Bruce sat by the fire smoking, and one by one they decided to turn in for the day.

Day Thirty-one

Dawn came in a clear sky, and a light wind blew from the southwest as Bruce awoke. He looked at Curt in the shelter, then glanced around to Jan in her hammock to his right. Both were sleeping soundly as he rose quietly, lit a cigarette, and walked down to the waterline. The sea carried very little motion, and waves seemed to just swish at the shore. He looked northward into unlimited visibility and watched idly at several gulls winging their way about in a calm sky. While he watched the horizon, thin slivers of cirrus clouds moved into view and contrasted the deep blue canopy above. Another weather system beginning, he thought, and that's about all we have to do, watch changes in the elements.

Bruce squatted down on the beach and continued to stare at the horizon until Jan's voice startled him. "Ryan, why all of the seclusion? Just couldn't sleep any longer, huh?"

He laughed. "Yeah, I guess I got up for that cup of java, but, alas, no java," he replied and reached for a cigarette. He extended the package but she shook her head.

"I think we all had a letdown after the radio transmissions didn't bring some results," she ventured.

"Yeah, and it showed on us. I was thinking about firing the set up a couple of times today. Do you suppose there'll be any Sunday drivers around somewhere?"

"You can never tell. There's a lot of military flying out of Hawaii every day. I've seen gaggles of Navy planes several times on Sunday during my layover flights," she replied.

They decided to return to camp and prepare breakfast. Curt joined them and the three sat making small talk into mid-morning. Bruce looked at the windmill and saw that it was rotating very little. "Folks, I think we should take a stab at broadcasting again. Probably useless, but what the heck. It can't hurt anything but our feelings when we don't get a reply," he said.

The broadcast went unanswered, but some scratchy static crackled on the receiver after he finished. He tried again in mid-afternoon with the same results. More cirrus clouds moved into the sky above them, and the survivors passed the remaining hours quietly. Darkness came shortly after they finished eating, and all three sacked out early.

Day Thirty-two

Gloom hung over Shoe Island as the sun rose and a brisk wind lashed at its palm trees. Later, dark clouds blocked out the sky completely, and thick haze limited visibility to about three miles or less. Bruce waited until twelve-thirty to make his broadcast, and static crackled on the receiver as he waited for a reply that never came. The afternoon brought little change except the wind velocity that increased from the southeast, and occasionally light sprinkles dripped down upon the lava haven.

All through the night wind continued to lash at the small island and rain started to cascade upon it intermittently. The ocean became verbal with huge waves crashing onto the beach and hammering at the lava barriers. Even birds sought refuge from the turbulent elements. Fitful sleep was all the survivors could manage while they huddled under the skimpy shelter and listened to sounds around them.

Day Thirty-three

Daylight brought no changes to the island, and it soon became obvious that a severe storm was moving across the area. Thunder rumbled and vivid lightning flashed continuously in the northwest sky. A southeast wind increased to gale force and palms began shedding limbs and coconuts regularly. The windmill rotated at its fastest rate ever, and the shelter appeared to be on the brink of collapsing.

"Folks, this is a real Pacific blow," Curt offered, "and it won't surprise me if we get soaking wet before it passes."

"Well, I guess I'd better move the radio gear to the center here and put the coverlets over it. Of course, it would get the bedding material, but it doesn't look like we'll be sleeping much more anyway," Bruce said.

"I just hope the shelter holds together. Going without sleep is one thing, but getting wet is another," Jan said.

Bruce noted that the windmill was rotating very fast even though the wind was coming from the southeast. Rain intensity increased, thunder boomed and lightning cracked sharply when it struck a palm tree near the spa. Then the wind shifted around to the northwest abruptly and the windmill crashed to the ground with a thud.

"That's all we need now!" Bruce said and looked down as he slapped the earth with his hand.

"Only three of the blades are bent. It doesn't look very bad from here," Jan said and turned away.

"Bruce, we'd better get something over the generator. The rain probably won't hurt it, but it could," Curt said.

He took the sailcloth to cover it and darted back inside. "It doesn't look like there's much damage. I think it's just a matter of rigging the bamboo poles again, and we'll be back in business. The blades aren't torn, only bent," Bruce said.

"As long as they're fairly straight, I think they'll do the job, all we want them to do is turn. A little wobble won't hurt," Curt added.

Heavy rain and gusty winds from the northwest continued, and a few branches blew off the shelter roof, but it remained intact. After thirty minutes the rain began diminishing and it finally stopped. Cloud cover lifted and thinned to the northwest, and the sun was shining brightly within another hour.

Jan and Bruce went about gathering and preparing their evening meal and they finished just before darkness fell. "A small fire would be nice," he said finally, "but I forgot to replenish my firewood inside the shelter, so everything is sopping wet. I guess we don't do any fireside chatting tonight."

"Oh well, there's always tomorrow night," Jan said.

"Yeah, one miss won't hurt anything," Curt added.

Day Thirty-four

Bruce awoke early with dread on his mind. What if I can't repair those blades. I could go back to the A-26 and get some of the skin aluminum and start over. That'll take another full day. But it looks like we have more time than anything else, he thought and looked over at Curt, then to Jan. They were both still asleep. Suddenly he became aware of the crispness in the air and decided there was actually a slight chill hanging over their island. He looked northward at a clear sky as far as he could see.

Curt raised up to look at Bruce but didn't speak after he saw that Jan was still sleeping. He took his crutch and ambled off to the john. Bruce lit a cigarette and started toward the beach. "Darn it, Ryan, why did you let it turn cold?" Jan said.

"Oh, just to make you uncomfortable. You know, boys will be boys and all that good stuff," he replied and they laughed.

"Do you think the windmill is ruined?" she asked.

"Nah, it looks like the fall bent those three blades, but the gen didn't touch the sand. I think I'll be able to repair it fairly easy."

"If you want to start on that right away, I'll gather some coconuts for breakfast. They should be easy to find, I heard them falling steadily last night due to the wind," she said.

"Okay, thanks. I'll get with it."

Curt came up as Bruce was cutting cord to anchor the generator to the bamboo stand, then he set it aside on the vinyl strip that had covered its housing. "How much damage do we have?" he asked.

"Not as much as I thought. The three blades are bent as you can see, and the wire connections pulled loose, but everything else looks good. I'll have to take the blades off and straighten them. Maybe by that time the wind will come back around from the south and west so we don't lose much more time."

"I don't know what I can do, but if you think of anything, just sing out and I'll do it," Curt offered.

"Nah, that won't be necessary. It's more a matter of time than anything else. One of the poles will have to be reworked, then Jan and I will get it back upright. Shouldn't be too much trouble. She's gathering some coconuts for breakfast. Guess that's our next move," Bruce replied.

After they ate, Bruce began working on the windmill by disassembling the shaft fittings. Once the blades were removed, he hammered them into shape using a tree trunk for an anvil. Next he reassembled them and saw that they rotated evenly. Then he retied a bamboo pole to complete the mast and lashed the generator in place. The day had slipped away rapidly. As twilight arrived, he and Jan were struggling to raise the windmill into the same position as it was before. Finally their task was completed and he turned to her. "Miss Adams, thanks for your good help, I couldn't have done it without you!"

"Mr. Ryan, it was my pleasure," she said and giggled.

Bruce chuckled and reached to spin the motionless blades.

Chapter Fourteen

Day Thirty-five

During the night, winds shifted to the southwest, and after dawn Bruce noted the windmill was turning over at a good rate. He left camp while his companions slept and walked to the beach, aware of dryness in the air and a very high, thin layer of cirrus clouds above. Ambling along the beach, smoking, he suddenly had an idea. "Maybe we're too conservative in using the radio only when we expect an airplane," he thought. "As soon as Jan and Curt are awake, I'm going to turn on the set and give it a whirl. We haven't had any luck with the airliners. It can't hurt to try."

While they munched coconut meat for breakfast, Bruce discussed his idea with Jan and Curt. "I think it's a great idea. Could be a military bird up there somewhere at most anytime. A lot of them leave their base early in the morning," Curt said.

"Once when I was in Honolulu, I think every aircraft on Hickam Field took off at daybreak. Everyone in the hotel was awakened because they kept circling the city for some reason, and the best I recall it was about mid-week," Jan added.

"Well, since we all agree it's worth a try, why don't I light that critter and speak my piece?" Bruce said and they laughed.

He snapped the receiver on first to a slight static crackle and readjusted the dial to 3023.5, then turned the volume down all the way. The transmitter made a solid click and, "Mayday! Mayday! Mayday! This is Am-Mex flight 755 survivors. Does anyone read? Over."

There was only a hum on the receiver when he turned the volume back up. Bruce repeated his call, then waited a minute to retransmit it. As he waited for the next minute to lapse, his thumb moved to the mike key, but before he reached the receiver volume knob, "Uh, Am-Mex 755 survivors, Canadian Air Force 458 here, do you read me?" the voice with a heavy French accent said.

Three hearts on Shoe Island froze in mid-beat.

"Canadian Air Force 458, I read you loud and clear. How me?" Bruce responded excitedly.

"Seven-five-five survivors, you are five-by-five, what is your message? Over."

"Four-five-eight, there are three of us. Janice Adams, Curtis Myrick, and Bruce Ryan. We're on a small island somewhere south and east of Hawaii. We ditched in Am-Mex flight 755 on March 24th and reached this island the next day."

"Seven-five-five, what is your survival situation now? Over."

"Two of us in good, one in fair condition. Food and water supplies are excellent, no other problems, over."

"Where did you obtain the radio equipmen? Over."

"We're using the radio from Captain Kenneth Kyle's aircraft that crashed here during the war. He's a Congressional Medal of Honor winner who has been missing since 1945. His crew members were Steven Grumfeld and Harry Harwood."

"Roger, on the equipment and names. Can you narrow your position down some. Anything at all will be of assistance, over."

"There is an airline flying Constellations that passes about twenty miles north of our position at 12:30 P.M. Pacific Time heading west on Monday, Wednesday, and Friday. They return eastward on Tuesday, Thursday, and Saturday about ten-thirty A.M., probably in and out of Honolulu. I estimate this island to be two miles long and it is shaped similar to a lady's high heel shoe. That's about all we can offer at this time, over."

"Roger, 755. We shall pass this contact to the American authorities immediately. I do not understand how you are speaking to us. We are at 25,000 feet over Vancouver, British Columbia at the moment."

"Four-five-eight, it's really good to hear your voice, and we want to thank you for reporting this for us, over."

"Oui, monsieur. Perhaps you know, your word 'mayday' comes from the French language. It is *m'aidez*, which means 'help me.' We are pleased to oblige. Good luck and someone will be coming for you very soon, over."

"That's the best news we've heard in more than a month, four-five-eight. We'll monitor this frequency on the hour and until a quarter past for any further transmissions. Thanks again for your help."

"Roger. Over and out."

"We made it! We made it! Contact with the outside world. But I don't know if I'm dreaming. Over Canada and they heard our broadcast!" Jan exclaimed and cupped her face in her hands.

"No, you're not dreaming! It's amazing! I've heard Navy pilots say during the war they picked up transmissions over the Pacific that originated from as far away as Australia. Some kind of skip due to atmospheric conditions," Curt said.

"Yeah, every once in a while I've heard similar things on radio in Houston. I guess this is just our lucky day. Is everybody ready to go home?" Bruce asked excitedly.

"I vote a resounding 'yes'!" Jan said and they all laughed.

"Me too, and I think the first thing I'll do when we get out of here is find a cup of mud. But I suppose the next thing is to get up to the spa, dunk myself and shave," Bruce said and they laughed happily.

"I guess we could all use a bath. It will be nice to get back to partake of some things we all take for granted. Bruce, if you'll help me up the Hump one more time, I'd appreciate it greatly," Curt said.

"You bet, whenever you want to go. How about now? I heard the gusher running a little while ago, then I can get on a schedule to monitor the frequency later."

"While you two do that, I'll round up some lunch. I don't think I'll be ordering crab anytime soon after we get back. The dunking sounds nice, and I might even wash my hair once more, for the last time," Jan added, giggling.

After they finished with baths and lunch, Bruce began tinkering with the radio equipment. The battery maintained good power and he looked to see if the windmill was still rotating. It was, in a steady breeze from the southwest. But there was no traffic on the receiver for the entire fifteen minutes he left it on. He noted the time of two-fifteen. "Well, that does it for another hour. I'll watch the ol' timepiece and fire it up again at three," he said.

Another hour dragged by, and Bruce turned the receiver on, but again there was no indication of traffic, only the steady hum of the equipment. He flipped the toggle switch to its off position and lit a cigarette. "I guess I'm rushing things a little. It has been only seven hours since we talked to the aircraft. Maybe I expected someone to show up immediately," he said.

"We're all anxious, and that makes the waiting seem longer and far more difficult," Curt offered.

"Yes, it does. But rescue wheels are turning out there somewhere and it won't be as long as it has been," Jan added.

At four-ten, Bruce heard scratchy static begin on the receiver, then after a moment, "Am-Mex 755 survivors, this is Air Force 13366, do you read? Over," the voice said in a decidedly Southern drawl.

"Air Force 13366, this is 755 survivors. I read you loud and clear, over," Bruce responded.

"I'd say that pilot is proficient in Dixiese," Curt quipped.

"Yes, he's definitely not from Brooklyn," Jan said and added, "but he sure does sound good!"

"Seven-five-five survivors, I'm now about four hundred miles out of Hickam trying to pinpoint your location. The Peruvian airline that operates the Connies gave us an approximate position based on your time frames. So far, I haven't seen an island like you described. I'm a Fox five-one at eleven thousand feet. Have you heard my engine noise at your position?"

"That's negative," Bruce said.

"Okay, folks, just stand by. I still have another fifty to a hundred miles range before I have to turn back. There was a little weather system hanging over the Hawaiians, so search and rescue sent me out to find your island before launching the amphibs. We understand there are no pressing survival problems right now, correct?"

"Three-six-six, that's affirmative. We're doing good, just anxious to get back to civilization."

"Yeah, I know what you mean. I'll continue southeast, and if you hear my engine, sing out. Aah, do you by chance have a signal mirror available."

"Affirmative, 336, and a flare pistol."

"Okay, when you hear the engine, give me a direction to turn to, or if you can see the plane, flick the mirror or fire a flare. I'll be able to see those quicker. Visibility is unlimited up here."

"Roger, 336, and what is the correct time?" Bruce said.

"It's two-fifteen Hawaiian Time."

Bruce reset his watch, and at two-thirty Jan was standing on the beach with a mirror in one hand and the flare pistol in the other as she scanned the horizon from east to west and back again.

After a moment, "Bruce, I can hear the Mustang's engine off to the northeast and I'm working the mirror, but I can't see the aircraft," she yelled.

"Three-six-six, you are to the northeast of our location. We can hear the engine but can't see the bird yet."

"Okay, survivors, I'm turning southwest now. Signal with the mirror and let me know every minute or so about the engine noise direction."

Jan fired the flare pistol and a blob of bright green arched into the sky, then she began flicking the mirror about to catch the sun's rays.

"Hey! I've got your island in sight. I'll be there shortly."

The F-51 came over Shoe Island and began a lazy circle. "Okay, folks, I've got this position logged on my grid sheet. I'd come down for a look-see, but I don't want to burn the extra fuel climbing back up. If everything is okay, I'll head back to Hickam and get the amphibs on their way first thing in the morning. You're four hundred miles southeast of Hawaii, or seventy-five miles farther out than search and rescue figured when they looked for you last month."

"Three-six-six, that sounds great to us, and we'll be ready to go when the plane gets here."

"You folks really have the media in a big stir over finding Captain Kyle's aircraft. The search and rescue coordinator said he already had a thousand calls at least from the news people since the Canadian pilot reported your contact. By the way, where on the island is the B-26?"

"Three-six-six, it's on the northwest corner. Near the top of the shoe's heel."

The Mustang banked into another half circle. "I guess I'm up too high, I can't see the Invader. Hang on, we'll be here to get you off tomorrow, rain or shine," the pilot said and left with a wing wave.

Bruce noted the radio's power supply was weakening and turned both units off. "I guess we'd better let the battery charge some now, the seaplane boys might want to talk with us in the morning."

"This all just seems unreal. I can't believe it's come to be so simple. A couple of days ago I thought we'd never get off this dune," Jan said and giggled while tears ran down her cheeks.

"We were all probably thinking the same thing, but once the word gets out, those search and rescue folks will go an extra ten miles to pluck someone out of the briny," Curt responded.

"I can't decide which made me the happiest. The Canadian pilot's voice or seeing that F-51 whizzing around overhead," Bruce added.

"It's no contest, the Mustang won going away," Jan said.

"A bird *over* the hand, huh?" Curt responded.

"Yes, indeed! That was a gorgeous sight to me."

Bruce lit a cigarette and took a long pull, then blew out a heavy plume of smoke. "Even these lousy cigs taste better now that it's a matter of hours. Folks, I think our luck has changed. I'm going down to catch a bunch of fish for supper," he said.

"That sounds like optimism if I've ever heard it, so I'll get some of the staples to add to them and skip the crab," Jan said and smiled.

Bruce laughed and went to get the fishing gear.

"Folks, if you don't mind, I think I'll take an APC and sack out for a little while," Curt said.

"Sure, go ahead. We'll give you a ring when supper is ready," Jan said and left to get the other foodstuff.

Bruce caught five fish large enough for their meal, and as they lingered around the fireside, darkness fell. A three-quarter moon rose and bathed the small island in its light. Later they bedded down. But just as children awaiting Christmas morning, sleep continued to evade them all. Finally, in the morning's first hours,

Bruce heard Curt snoring lightly and Jan turn again in her hammock. He felt a sigh escape his lips and then fell asleep.

Day Thirty-six

The sun had risen above puffy, golden clouds when Bruce awoke with a start. He looked and saw Curt sitting up in the shelter and that Jan had left her hammock. "I guess we all slept in this morning. Jan got up just a few minutes ago," Curt said.

Bruce lit a cigarette and checked the time. It was seven o'clock. "Yeah, I thought I'd never fall asleep last night. Wonder what kind of bird they'll send for us. A PBY?" he said.

"I don't know, really, but kind of doubt a PBY. I haven't seen any of those around in quite a while."

"Well, any kind will beat what we've had, huh?"

"Yeah, it sure will," Curt replied.

"Looks like we're all up and waiting but not very patiently," Jan said as she walked up to the shelter with three coconuts. "And here's breakfast for everyone."

"We sure can't complain about the room service, but I don't think I'll be in the market for any more coconuts for a while," Bruce said and laughed. Jan and Curt joined him as they all went from the shelter area to the firesite to eat.

Bruce saw the time was approaching eight, and went over to turn the receiver on for the next quarter hour. There was no traffic to monitor and he switched the set off at eight fifteen. If an aircraft left at six, he thought, and most of those amphibs fly at 150-175 knots, it should take about three hours to get here. Around nine is right.

Jan came up to him. "Bruce, do you think we'll need the mirrors this time?" she asked.

"Nah, they know where we are, and I thought I'd turn the radio on at eight forty-five to see if they're calling us. That's my guess for an ETA."

"I can't wait to see that aircraft in our lagoon. It's like, maybe, they could decide not to come at all," she said.

He laughed. "Aah, don't worry, they're coming," he said and reached out to squeeze her hand.

She smiled and ambled toward the beach.

Bruce flipped both units on at eight forty-five. "Air Force rescue, this is Am-Mex 755 survivors, do you read? over," he began and turned the receiver volume up.

"Am-Mex 755 survivors, this is Air Force 15282, reading you loud and clear, how me?"

"Air Force 15282, five-by-five, what's your position?"

"We estimate twenty to twenty-five minutes out. We're a flight of two SA-16s at 5500 feet. What's your status, over?"

"We're doing okay, just anxious for your arrival."

"Hang on, we're coming with hot meals, coffee, cigarettes, all the comforts of home. For a direction finding bearing, key your transmitter for one minute."

Bruce pressed the mike button for a minute and remained silent so their receiver could pinpoint the area where his transmission was coming from. Then he said, "All of those goodies sound great to us and we're standing by."

"We have the island in sight. I'll call back shortly about a landing area."

Drumming of the Albatrosses' engines sent Jan scurrying to the waterline, and as the planes descended lower she began waving with both hands.

The SA-16s banked left after passing overhead and continued to the east a short distance. "Hello, survivors, 282. The lagoon in front of the person on the beach appears to be a good zone to taxi into once we're down, do you agree."

"Affirmative, 282. There are no submerged objects in that area, we crossed it perfectly in our raft. To the west, there's a section of lava underwater. I'll get the lady to stand at its edge, and everywhere east of her will be clear of obstacles. The wind is southwest, estimated ten miles an hour, and the altimeter is 29.92."

"Roger. You sound like a regular tower man."

"In the flesh. Old habits are hard to break," Bruce said, then called to Jan for her to move next to the barrier's edge on the beach.

The aircraft continued in a wide circle to the east and north, then approached the island to touch down in trail. They lowered their landing gear in the water, taxied onto the beach and swung back heading to the sea before stopping the engines. Crewmen exited by a hatch over the wheel wells. A medic went over to Jan with his medical kit, but she hugged him briefly and sent him on to Curt.

Two men from the nearest plane carried a large container resembling a covered serving tray. The pilots were last out, and Jan rushed to hug them both while everyone grinned. From the distant plane, movie and still photographers hurriedly emerged with their equipment moving and clicking in every direction.

Bruce had switched off the radio equipment earlier and went forward to greet Sergeant Lucas, a blonde, stocky medic, while he checked Curt over with a brief, preliminary exam.

The pilot of plane 282 introduced himself to Jan, Bruce, and Curt as John Fisher and explained that he coordinated rescue missions as a primary duty, but since he missed them back on 24 March, he just had to make this one in person. Then he insisted that the three survivors eat some of the food they had brought. He got no opposition from any of them.

"Major, I love coffee, and must have drunk fifty gallons of it in the last year alone. But this absolutely *has* to be the best cup of mud I've ever had anywhere!" Bruce said as they began eating.

"Ryan, just a week or so ago you were telling me all about some kind of battery acid the military *always* serves as coffee," Jan quipped.

"Aah, they had to pick this up in Honolulu," he countered as the assembled group laughed.

The aircrew looked about the island while the survivors finished their meal. Then the pilot of Air Force 15291, Lieutenant Joe Edkins, an average size man with black hair, began speaking. "Mr. Ryan, I flew the other plane down to recover the remains of Captain Kyle and his crew. Could you tell or show us where they are?"

"Call me Bruce, Lieutenant Edkins, and yeah, I'll show you. The aircraft is on the other side of the lava dome. There is a way to walk around it, but I think it would be simpler to just taxi your bird out a hundred yards, then around to the site. The shore next to the A-26 is just like this one and you won't have any trouble beaching there. I've wrapped the remains in a chute and secured them with the risers, so they'll be easy to remove."

"Okay, Bruce, call me Joe. It sounds like a good idea to taxi around. When you're ready, we'll be off."

"This is Sergeants Diehl and Brush from Graves Registration. They have all of the necessary equipment to take care of the remains." Diehl raised his hand in a wave and said, "Dick," while Brush followed suit and said, "Jerry." Both men were small in stature with light brown hair. As they prepared to leave, the major's copilot, a lieutenant, walked up and indicated that he wanted to go with them. "Bruce, I'm Eddie O'Brien. With so many names being thrown around, I thought I'd better repeat mine," the tall, slim redhead offered.

"Thanks, I'm terrible on names anyway," Bruce said, extending his hand as the others chorused agreement.

They boarded the SA-16 and Joe started one engine to taxi around to the top of the shoe's heel. Ten minutes later the aircraft beached, and they all exited and walked the short distance to the A-26. The photographers were filming busily again and insisted that Bruce pose beside the aircraft. "Hey, gentlemen, I'm just a Johnny-come-lately. Jan actually found the bird," Bruce protested.

"Well, we'll get some more pictures with her after their caskets are covered with flags. She indicated back there that she didn't want to take part in this operation at all. The other gentleman doesn't appear up to it, and one of you has to take credit," Brush said and smiled.

Bruce went over to stand by the A-26 for a moment, then each of the men assisted in removing Ken, Steve, and Harry from the bomber and placed them into the SA-16. "Earl, I've heard some about such crashes and all, but what will they do with these weapons that are on the Invader?" Bruce asked after they finished and closed the canopy back.

"We have a special crew that will come back, probably in another week or so. They will remove the weapons and all useable parts from Air Force, uh, Army 34518, then show it on the A-26 salvaged roster," he replied.

The medic checked Curt again briefly after he had eaten, then went to the spa for a water sample that would be tested later for its contents. All of the crewmen were engaged in other activities, and

Jan went over to Curt. "What did the medic tell you? Good news, I hope," she said.

"Well, he said that he wasn't a doctor first, but thought I'd had a light stroke and possibly ruptured a blood vessel in my brain. They have tests to determine damage and that sort of thing. He did say, too, that I have youth on my side; where an older person may not ever recover, my chances are good," he replied.

"That's great news, of a sort at least, and they're making large strides in medical technology these days. I've heard that the hospital at Hickam is one of the best in our military services. Maybe they'll check you over there first and then the civilians will know better how to treat your problem," she said.

"Jan, I have to tell that major about what I did to you, and when we get to Hawaii go to the civil authorities with it," Curt said.

"Curt, no!" she exclaimed in a low voice. "You weren't in control of your faculties then. I know that now. Earlier, I had doubts, but not anymore. It's dead and buried here. If you tell it, that would embarrass me terribly, and I'll have to say you were unconscious three days and must have fantasized it. Please! Forget it and let's celebrate our rescue plus the discovery of those three heroes in the bomber."

John came up to them then. "Well, people, we're almost ready to take you three back to civilization. I heard Joe fire his engine a moment ago and they should be here shortly. Is there anything that you wish to carry back from here?"

"There's nothing here that I cherish, although I'm grateful for the survival conditions it provided. But it isn't my favorite place to be. Bruce will want his AWOL bag, I know!" Jan replied and smiled.

"Nothing for me, major," Curt said.

"We have photos of most everything, the campsite, shelter, radio gear, the whole works. I'll see that you get copies of those in case you want souvenirs. I had one of the crewmen deflate your raft, and we'll take that back to Am-Mex. We have its picture too," John said.

"Good, it served us well. The survival items really helped, not only with supplies but kept us out of the sea. That was the worst storm I've ever seen and I thought we were goners several times that first night. But it carried us through," Jan offered.

"You weren't the only one. I've seen storms and then some, but that was a monster and it really carried us a long way with it. You're right, the raft was our salvation," Curt added.

Joe taxied Air Force 291 in and beached it as before. Then Bruce joined the group flying in Air Force 282. "Major, I think I'll use the raft's coverlets for the radio gear and generator. Earl told me a salvage crew would come back soon to get the weapons and useable parts from the bomber," Bruce said.

"Yes, that's a good idea. No use in letting perfectly good equipment ruin. After all, it got you three off this sand dune," John replied. "Incidentally, you call it 'Shoe Island.' That's a good name, we'll show it on our charts and reports," he added.

All personnel got on board and the SA-16s took off. John and Joe coordinated their operations briefly by radio, then circled back over the small island at one thousand feet and flew along its entire length. In Air Force 282, Jan, Bruce, and Curt gazed down intently at what was their home for thirty-five days. From the cockpit, John looked back at his passengers, smiled, and did a mild wing wave. Joe followed his lead. Ken, Steve, and Harry probably approved of it, too.

The two hour and forty-five minute flight was uneventful, but as Fisher taxied from the runway to the parking ramp, Jan became frantic. "Ryan, find your AWOL bag and get the comb. I see two dozen photographers standing out there waiting to meet us. My hair has to be a fright!"

All of the men laughed and assured her the hairdo was appropriate for anyone being rescued. The press corps snapped countless pictures and asked dozens of questions for fifteen minutes, then John insisted that the survivors leave for the hospital and their checkups. The journalists left to track down the crew of Air Force 291 who were removing the remains of the three bomber crewmen for transportation to a local morgue.

A staff car came and carried Jan, Bruce, and Curt to the base hospital where they were ushered into showers, fresh clothing, and to a steak luncheon. As the meal concluded, a willowy, brunette nurse with a major's insignia on her uniform greeted them. "Welcome to Hickam Air Force Base and to civilization. I'm Shirley Marshall, and I'll be your host during your stay here," she said and her light brown eyes seemed to sparkle.

The three introduced themselves and Bruce began. "Major, you said during our stay here. I'm several weeks late for work. Maybe I should get on over to Honolulu International, or they could send me back to Houston on the next boat. Make that a slow boat!"

Everyone laughed. "Mr. Ryan, we have a research program in progress for survivors of air and sea mishaps of more than seven days' duration. We take their medical histories and determine what they did to help themselves. Major Fisher radioed a preliminary report to us on what you told him en route. We have contacted and gotten permission from the CAA, Am-Mex, and Click Airlines to keep you here for three days for physicals, which you need, and to record your experiences—if you agree to it! I hope you will. This could help others in the future who face your same circumstances. It's without charge to you, and some of our best people will be studying all aspects of this situation," she replied.

"Well, call me Bruce, and if the CAA has no objections, then neither do I. I'll stay if you'll agree to furnish more of that coffee Major Fisher brought with him," he said.

They all laughed. "Count me in. I'd like to know what's going on inside my head. The sooner the better. Call me Curt."

"I'm Shirley, and we have a great neurosurgeon on staff. He'll give you a good work up very soon. In fact, he wants to see you shortly and begin some preliminary tests for your case," she said.

"Call me Jan and I'll stay too, if you have an innerspring mattress and a phone so I can talk with my parents."

"Great! I'm glad you're all staying. You'll be in private rooms with *innerspring* mattresses. You're allowed one call each to the mainland at our expense. I'll make the arrangements now and check back shortly to get started," Shirley said and left the room.

During the afternoon Curt underwent tests to determine the extent of his injuries. Jan and Bruce had brief physicals to check for possible diseases they might have acquired. Then they filled out questionnaires and had interviews about their experiences. Both received good reports on their condition, and before the evening meal Shirley led them to an office where they could place calls to their relatives.

"I'm sure every newspaper, radio, and television station on the mainland has your complete story by now, but there's nothing like hearing it from the horse's mouth when a relative has been missing for as long as you all were. Calls are limited to ten minutes, so talk fast, then go to the dining room and eat as much as you want. And Bruce, that includes coffee," Shirley said and left smiling.

They finished the telephone calls and went to the diner for supper. Curt was already there and greeted them warmly. Major Fisher came in with three sets of photographs from Shoe Island as he promised. He also gave them a copy of the local newspaper with a headline shouting about the recovery of Ken Kyle's crew. A subtitle emphasized the rescue of Jan, Bruce, and Curt.

Each of them pored over the accounts and pictures of their ordeal. Photographs of Ken, Steve, and Harry were included with the articles.

"Hmmm, that Ken was a good-looking hombre, and it's too bad he didn't survive the war. But I'm glad we found him. At least his family can now put him to rest," Jan said.

"Ken was an elite football player. There was a joke in the East about several coaches sending gifts to him when he graduated from West Point," Bruce added.

Curt laughed. "And how are they treating you two here?" he asked.

"Excellent," said Jan, and Bruce agreed.

"Did you get to call your folks yet?" Bruce asked.

"Yeah, I spoke with my dad, and he said the media was really buzzing about us and Kyle. They knew we were all okay, but he was happy to talk with me personally. My ex is in Oke City and even she called him when the news broke. Sort of makes me feel good that she still remembers me," he said.

"Well, what do the medics say about your injury?" Jan asked.

"Not much so far. They have X-rayed my head from every possible angle imaginable and taken specimens for tests. The doc did say my left side looks good, very little deterioration, and if it's a broken vessel in my brain, they can probably repair it and restore movement and feeling to my limbs. He also mentioned a hospital in California that specializes in brain damage work. They want to do a little more here, and after they find the trouble, send me there."

"Sounds good. We'll both be pulling for you to make a full recovery. Just take it easy and hope for the best," Jan said.

"Yeah, man, they can do wonders for injuries now, and ironically, a whole lot of what has been learned came about as a result of the war. Those battlefield hospitals pulled off some miracles I heard. Right now, I'm looking forward to sacking out on a soft pad for a change. Good night, folks. See you tomorrow," Bruce added.

Chapter Fifteen

Day Thirty-seven

The hospital seemed almost peaceful on Saturday morning as the survivors met for a leisurely breakfast before resuming their test sessions. "You know, I can't get used to this celebrity thing. I'm amazed at how many people have just come up to congratulate me and wish me well," Bruce said while they lingered over extra cups of coffee.

"Yes, everyone certainly has been nice. And some of them are nice *looking*," Jan said and giggled.

"I sure have a great doctor. He's even coming out today to do a special test for me. Some kind of probe or something. I can't ever remember medical terms. Anyway, it's suppose to tell him what all I will need down the road," Curt added.

Shirley and Sergeant Shwallon, a dark stocky medic, came to their table. "Okay, Bruce and Jan, it's back to paperwork for you. Curt, your doctor is here. The sergeant will take you to him," she said.

Jan and Bruce spent the morning going over actual case histories recorded by other survivors and comparing their experiences to those. Just before lunch time, Shirley came into the room.

"Christmas came early this year. An Am-Mex representative came by and left these checks for each of you. Three hundred bucks advanced clothing allowance. There's a staff car outside, and after lunch I'll take you to a department store so you can get some clothes to replace items that sank with your plane. Afterwards, more paperwork, okay?"

"Yes, that's fine. Thanks," Jan said and Bruce nodded. "Is Curt coming with us?" she added.

"No, he's a little shaky from his tests, and he had already called someone to bring some things to him," Shirley began. "All of the families of the bomber crewmen have expressed delight that you three wore their son's uniforms. Steve's family asked that we dress him in the one that Curt wore. We complied. Jan, yours is on Harry, and Bruce's is on Ken. Of course, they were run through the GI laundry first," she added and smiled.

"By golly, it was an honor for me to wear Ken's uniform, and I'll contact his family to tell them when I get out of here," Bruce said.

"It would be nice if all three of us sent them some kind of message like that, I think," Jan added.

"Yes, it would, and I know they'll appreciate it. President Truman ordered their remains be flown home to Maryland, and they're on the way this morning. There should be quite a reception awaiting them in Baltimore tonight."

"Oh, he also awarded Steve and Harry the Distinguished Service Medal, our second highest military award. All three of them were awarded a Distinguished Flying Cross and Air Medal. I thought that was very nice," Shirley said.

"That's great. It's very unusual that they are all from the same state. That didn't happen very often during the war," Bruce said.

"Yes, the media has made a huge thing of it, and Governor Lane proclaimed a mourning period from now until their funerals are held—with full military honors, of course," Shirley said.

"Well, I can't wait to get downtown for the shopping spree. Don't drag around, Ryan. Be ready to go right after lunch!" Jan said and giggled loudly.

"One o'clock sharp in front of the hospital," Shirley added, pointing her finger at Bruce and smiled.

After two hours of shopping, they returned to the base and resumed their project work. "We'll continue this part of the program until chow time, then stop until tomorrow," Shirley said.

After sitting in silence for a while, Jan said, "You know, this is similar to aptitude tests I had on job applications and in college. A lot of the items have more than one answer."

"Yeah, the military got into the psychological business in a big way during the war. Aircrews played a heavy role in it, especially about fear while flying in combat and all that," said Bruce.

"The thing I noticed first is that they ask a question here, then a few lines later the same item comes up again, only with different phrasing. Here's one. Did you have any sexual urges at any time during your ordeal? Next, did you have a sexual encounter during this period of time? What does that have to do with survival?" she said and looked up to see that his cheeks were tinted pink.

"That's one you'll have to ask Shirley," he said as she giggled.

Curt joined Jan and Bruce for the evening meal and they discussed the aspects of their testing. Both noticed that he had a withdrawn look on his face and wasn't quite as alert as before. "Curt, you seem tired. Are the procedures painful or just fatiguing?" she asked.

"A little of both, I guess. The doctor told me today that he wanted me to sack out all day tomorrow and do some paperwork for them, a questionnaire thing, I don't know," he replied.

"There's nothing to it. That's what we've done most of the day, along with the specimen bit and blood pressure checks," Jan offered.

"Yeah, it's easy. You had a bunch of it in the Navy like I did in the Air Corps, uh, Force," Bruce said. "Okay folks, chow time's over now and I'm gonna sack out early. The shopping binge wiped me out."

As they departed the dining hall, Jan drew close to Curt and spoke in a low voice so that Bruce couldn't hear. "Curt, some things are very personal on those inventories. Remember what we discussed just before leaving Shoe Island. It's still dead and buried back there with the crab and the lava. Okay?"

"Your wish is my command. Although I don't agree, whatever you say is what it will be," he replied.

"Thanks, and have a great night."

"My pleasure, and you have a good one, too."

Day Thirty-eight

Sunday was even slower than Saturday at Hickam Air Force Base, but Shirley arrived right on time. "You people probably thought this tormentor was taking a day off today. Not so. But it won't be as hectic nor as long as the other two days. You're making good progress, the best we've had yet," she said and smiled.

"Shirley, just keep the coffee pot on, and I'll stick close all day," Bruce replied.

"If anyone loves coffee better than this guy, I've never seen them," Jan said and they all laughed.

Curt arrived in his wheelchair and Sergeant Shwallon parked him by their table. "How was the night?" Jan asked.

"Oh, it was good. I slept well and feel more rested than in the last couple of days. How about you?"

Each one reported having a pleasant night and being in good spirits this morning. Then Shirley prompted Jan and Bruce to get started on the final phase of their program. Curt said goodbye and asked the medic to return him to his room for the paperwork session.

The day passed slowly with lunch and dinner being welcome breaks for Jan and Bruce. Curt returned with them for the evening meal, and they discussed the questionnaires in detail. All agreed on the importance of the program and expressed the hope that their experiences might help someone else to survive in a hostile environment, once it was published into a survival manual and distributed.

Bruce chuckled. "I can just see people sitting in training sessions discussing this manual, half-asleep, and thinking, 'That will never happen to me.'"

"That sounds like the voice of experience, Bruce," Curt said, smiling.

"Yeah, I'm afraid it is. In flight school they taught us survival, first aid, weather, and all kinds of things that I didn't think were important. Before we got off Shoe Island, I wished that I'd paid more attention and tried to remember some of what they said."

Jan and Curt grinned. "Yes, I'm sure we have all been in that position at some point. The airline really stressed survival in our training, and without passing marks, girls were washed out of the program in a hurry," said Jan.

"The Navy and Click are both gung-ho on it too, especially things pertaining to the sea. But then, they're more directly involved with it than the Army," Curt added.

He then signaled to the medic that he was ready to leave, and they all retired to their rooms for the evening.

Day Thirty-nine

Bruce was on his third cup of coffee when Jan and Curt joined him for breakfast. A young airman strode up to their table. "Mr. Ryan, you have an overseas call in Major Marshall's office, just down the hall, sir."

"Did they say who it was?"

"No sir, I'm sorry, they didn't."

"Okay, thanks very much," Bruce said as he hurried out.

He picked up the phone and spoke his name.

"Honey, I hope I'm not disturbing you there, but I just *had* to call and wish you a happy birthday," Carolyn Ryan said.

"Aah, mom, you're an angel to think of me. Thanks a bunch, but you shouldn't have gone to all this trouble."

"Trouble! It's no trouble! I only picked up the phone. Are you all right? You're sick or hurt and they just aren't telling me."

"No, mom, I'm fine. Like I told you Friday, I have no problems at all. We're supplying information to try and help someone else in case they wind up like we did. You know, a survival training program."

"Well, you don't sound very good. There's something, I see it in your face when they show the pictures of you on television."

"Aah, mom, I'm fine, really! These transoceanic lines are the problem, in fact, you sound almost like a kid yourself."

"Okay, you take care and have a nice birthday. Write to us as soon as you can. I love you!"

"Thanks, Mom. I love you, too. I'll be out of here tomorrow and will get in touch with you and Dad then, okay?"

"Bye."

Just then, Jan walked into the major's office. "Not bad news, I hope."

Bruce grinned. "Nah, it was Mama. She called to wish her baby boy a happy birthday."

"Now that was sweet of her."

"Yeah, she's a real doll. Never forgets."

"Never forgets what?" Shirley said as she came into the office.

"Today is Bruce's birthday, and his mom called him a few minutes ago to wish him a happy one," Jan replied.

"That's nice, and happy birthday from the Air Force. How many is this, about eighteen?" Shirley said and smiled.

He laughed. "Yeah, eighteen at least and no more than twenty-four, just a kid really."

"The ripe old age of twenty-four," Jan said and leaned over to peck his cheek. "Have a happy one."

"Thank you, ladies, and now I guess we need to get on to more important things like survival surveys and all that good stuff, huh?"

"Right, the show must go on," Shirley said.

They spent the morning on the paperwork project, then broke for lunch. Bruce had a cupcake with one candle on it when they got to the dining room.

During the afternoon each survivor went for physical checks and specimen collection. Curt joined them shortly before dinner.

"How did your exam go?" Jan asked.

"Well, the doctor said I have a small vein broken in the right side of my brain, and he thinks that repairing it will restore most of the use of my limbs. But there was some 'cloudiness' in the X-rays and he wasn't sure just how much damage had been done. I told him about drinking the coconut milk, and he said it was surprising that it didn't do more damage than it did."

"What does he mean by that?" Bruce asked.

"He said with that water heating, cooling, and reheating the juice was the same as distilling liquor. His guess is that the alcohol was at least 150 proof and maybe even 200. That combined with consuming it on an empty stomach almost did me in. He likened it to a strong surge of water going through a network of pipes. It came to a weak point and just blew it out. When I was ten years old I had a Shetland pony. I'd seen the Indians in movies run and jump on their horses bareback. I did that one day and it must have frightened the pony. He started running and went under a small tree. The limbs pushed me off his back and one of the rear hooves hit a glancing blow on the right side of my head. It knocked me out for a couple of days, and the doc feels this played a part in the situation."

"When will you know about surgery, or did the doctor discuss that with you yet?" Jan asked.

"Well, yes and no. He said the sooner the better, but he thinks I should go to California to the famous Vincent Medical Center and have a final test. That's what I intend to do. He's to call someone there about it soon," Curt replied.

"They do some great things now in medicine, and we'll be pulling for you to get that blowout fixed and back to rolling on all four wheels again soon," Bruce added.

"Yeah, thanks. You two be sure and stop in tomorrow before checking out. It'll be late tomorrow afternoon before I can leave for the mainland," Curt said.

They both agreed to come by. "Hey, it's chow time for sure. Let's eat, and don't forget, be sure and try the stuffed crab," Bruce jested.

Both of his companions groaned. They all laughed and Bruce pushed Curt's wheelchair for him. As they finished dinner, Major Fisher rushed into the dining hall to tell them there would be a special radio broadcast on the funerals of Ken and his crew shortly. They went to the hospital's day room to listen. Vice President Barkley gave a nice eulogy for the crewmen and presented their families with medals and flags. The newscast concluded with an update on the status of Jan, Bruce, and Curt in Hawaii.

Chapter Sixteen

Day Forty

Bruce had just begun his fourth cup of coffee when Jan came into the dining room for breakfast wearing a form-fitting, off-white suit with royal blue trim. "Hey, lady, that's a mighty sharp outfit you're wearing. You look so nice! These flyboys are gazing at you something fierce. And so am I," he said, and grinned.

She rolled her eyes upward and smiled as she set her tray on the table. "Thank you, I'm glad you like it. I had to let Am-Mex know I spent their loot for clothing. The rep will probably be there to check me out when I board the plane," she replied and sat down.

"Aah, you're gonna deadhead to the States today, then?"

"Yes. The company wants me back in Houston for some kind of promotional campaign they're planning. Then I'll resume my regular runs and rotation. By the way, Shirley is taking us to International Airport," Jan said.

"I talked with the tower chief earlier and he told me to just stop by, but I didn't have to report for work until I felt like it. Boy, what an open-ended racket that could turn into," Bruce joked as they were finishing breakfast.

Jan smiled. "Well, I'd better go back to the room and get my things together. May I see you privately a moment before we leave?"

"Yeah, you bet, shortly!" he said and left for his room. He gathered his toiletries quickly and zipped them into the AWOL bag. Then he piled his clothing and bag into a chair and left for Jan's room. He tapped lightly on the door and waited.

She opened it momentarily and he walked in past her. "Bruce, when you say shortly, you mean *shortly*. I hate goodbyes," she said and took his hands in hers. "But I wanted to say a special thanks for what you did for me. I'll always remember your many kindnesses. Now, I guess it's time to go," she added and kissed him lightly on the lips.

"Adams, that's why I hustled down here—to keep you from leaving."

"Huh? I have to, my job you know."

"That one is only temporary. There's a lifetime job for you here."

"Ryan, what on earth are you talking about?" she asked and laughed. "Oh! Is this a proposal of matrimony?"

"Yeah, it is."

"And it's because of what happened back on Shoe Island, isn't it?"

"Well, yeah."

"I thought so."

"But it first started when you welcomed us aboard Am-Mex flight 755. Then you said to me, 'Mr. Ryan, get your butt up there with that other guy, I want your seat.' It wus them blue eyes whut got me!"

She began laughing merrily. After a moment she stopped and looked into his eyes as he stood watching her with a broad grin on his face. "Bruce, you hardly know me. Five weeks, or is it six?"

"I've lost count, but that doesn't matter. We've been through more together in that time than most couples have in two years. I've never met a woman that I admire and respect more than you, except Mama."

"Well, I don't mind being second fiddle there. Thank you."

"You handled your first ditching like someone who had done it a dozen times. I was scared silly, but you and, who was the other girl?"

"Debbie."

"Yeah. I expected both of you to panic at any moment, as I was about to, but you didn't. Then in the raft and on the island, you did more than your part on every count. No griping about what we didn't have and no complaints when things really got tough."

"Yes, I did. After . . . I leaned on you heavily and you were so sweet and kind about that. Several times out there you held me and it probably saved my life. A shoulder to cry on was so

George A. Reynolds

important right then, I couldn't have made it any further without it!"

"Well, I can tell you now, I saw this exquisite mug, a nice, warm smile and relished your cute little digs at me every day. They kept me going. Several times I thought we'd never get off that rock, but somehow your disposition would always get me looking up again."

She continued to look into his eyes. "I don't understand why you waited until now to tell me this."

"Well, on the island when I realized that I loved you, I thought maybe you'd think like that old line, 'Way out here in the boonies, even the ugliest natives are beginning to look good to the troops.' Then I saw some flickers of affection, or camaraderie at least, from you. But I had to see if those held in civilization, too. I figured they'd send us to a Honolulu hospital when we got back, and I was on shaky ground with my figuring until the Air Force solved that problem for me. Then I decided to wait until the last day for my totem pole check. I guess it was because I suspected you'd politely say thanks, but no thanks, and I wanted to delay that as long as possible."

Jan was quaking with laughter. "Ryan, I've always heard there are young controllers and there are old controllers, but there are no old, sane controllers. How long have you been one, five years? I think you're a dab along already," she joked.

"Yeah, and most of it's from working rotating shifts. After a little while, one is sleepy at the table, hungry in bed, and amorous on the job. And I plead guilty, but I'm more crazy about this beautiful, life-size Texas doll."

She smiled. "Bruce, you know that I've been married and then there was the thing with Curt."

"I knew some girls before you. All of that is in our past. You're brand new as far as I'm concerned."

Jan continued looking into his eyes. "As you hugged me when we found the bomber, I felt your heart beating very strongly. Somehow it wasn't the same as with concern about my safety, but more like I hadn't gone away after all and was still there. Your hands were shaking like you were holding a girl for the first time. Then you kissed my cheek. I knew your feelings toward me weren't all platonic as you had been trying very hard to display. Every day afterward I found myself falling for you like a big bird with zero glide ratio. We left that totem pole back on Shoe Island."

"Do you really mean that?"

"Yes."

"And is your answer to my proposal the same?"

She nodded, "If you want me."

Bruce blocked her speech with a kiss. They stood in a prolonged embrace and kissed again. "Oh, yeah, I really do! There has been a dread on my mind for a long time about the prospects of life without you, and I've wanted to hold and kiss you a thousand times in the last two days alone."

"And I wanted you to, for weeks!" she responded.

"Well, we have from now on to make up for lost time," he said and started kissing her again.

"Hey! Cut that out! This *is* a research center, but we don't work with love bugs nor birds and bees. Anyway, it's time to travel," Shirley said and laughed as she entered the room.

They separated and snickered. "We were just practicing for when the preacher says, 'Kiss the bride' and all that good stuff," Bruce said.

"Kiss the bride? Is Jan going to be one?" Shirley asked.

"Yes, Bruce just proposed and I accepted," Jan said.

"Well, congrats, and June is almost here," Shirley replied.

"June! I was thinking of today," Bruce moaned.

"Today! Ryan, we can't possibly do it this soon. No planning, no license, no blood tests and all of that," Jan said.

"What's to plan? Just get the paper, show up and say I do," he countered.

"Boy! You're in a hurry! I knew it wouldn't be very long from the start." Shirley began. "Okay, Jan, I'll help you bag this sucker if that's what you want," she continued. "We routinely check all blood for cooties, and neither of you had any. We'll back date the certificates to 28 April when the blood was drawn. Normally, there's a three-day waiting period after a license is issued, but I know a nurse in the Territorial Bureau of Health. She'll date it that same day. In your case I can't see what difference a couple of days will make. What is your religious preference?" she asked.

"I'm Baptist," Jan replied.

"Me too," Bruce chorused.

"All right. Chaplain Arthur Franklin is a friend of mine. He's from McComb, Mississippi and about as Southern Baptist as you can get. I'm sure he'll perform the ceremony. I'll call to make arrangements with him and the bureau nurse. My car is outside, and as soon as I get the certificates done, we'll go get the license. Their office is only three miles down the road. Now, you two get out in the open where we can keep an eye on you and stand by a little while," Shirley said and smiled, then hurried out of the room.

"Bruce, are you sure about this? Any doubts at all?" Jan asked.

"I've never been as sure of anything before. Absolutely no doubts! How about you?"

"No, but neither of us is dressed for a wedding."

"Aah, it doesn't matter what people wear. Besides, if you look any better in something other than this outfit you have on, I don't think I could wait till dark to consummate the marriage," Bruce said, grinning.

Jan giggled, pulled on his ear and pushed him toward the door. "Ooh, a dirty old man already. Let's go to Shirley's office before a love bug comes in and bites us both."

"Okay. I hate wearing suits, but I did get a blue one, and for you, I'll put it on before we go to the chapel."

She smiled and they left for the office.

"Okay, kids, the certificates are done. Let's go get the other paperwork. Chaplain Franklin said he would be delighted to perform the ceremony, and he's making arrangements in the chapel. I hope you don't mind, but I called the public information officer, too. They want to do a story and get pictures of the event. You folks are going to be famous before this is over," Shirley said.

"Pictures. Oh, I knew this was too soon. I look a fright," Jan complained.

"Wrong! You look gorgeous in that outfit. We'll rig a headpiece, put a suit on this sucker and everything will be just fine," Shirley said and squeezed her hand.

"Rings!" Bruce exclaimed. "I don't have a ring."

"You're not getting out of this now, buster. I'll take you by the base exchange, then we'll get the license. Let's go," Shirley said.

After stopping at the base exchange for the rings, they started for the health office. "Are you married, Shirley?" Jan asked.

"No way. I'm a good Catholic and the oldest of ten kids. I grew up in Radcliff, Kentucky and had all of the snot-nose kids and diapers I could stand with my brothers and sisters. I love them dearly, but they made a believer out of me, and I'm not marrying until I'm too old to have brats of my own."

Jan and Bruce tittered. "I came to Hawaii to get away from home, is that why you're in the Air Force?" Bruce asked.

"You'd better believe it. I finished nursing school in '44 and the Army sent a nurse to explain the advantages of going into the military service. Of course, the war was still going on and I kind of wanted to help out, and no one else told me I could retire in twenty years either. That should be about the right time for me to get married," she replied and they all laughed.

After obtaining the license, they started for the chapel. "Oh my goodness. We didn't tell Curt about our plan, and I hope he understands the rush and all," Jan said.

"I'm sure he will, but why don't we go there first, Shirley, and invite him to go with us. Shouldn't take very long," Bruce said.

"Okay, suits me. That would be nice, if he's up to it," she replied.

Back at the hospital, they went to Curt's room and he was lying in bed but sat up when the trio came. "Well, my friend, Jan and I have some good news," Bruce said.

"Yeah, well I'm ready for some of that kind, speak on!" he said.

"Bruce and I are going to be married in just a few minutes, and we'd like for you to come with us. It's just a little way to the chapel. Are you feeling well enough?" Jan asked.

"Congratulations! I'm very happy for you both. I don't think either of you could have made a better choice for a mate. I know you'll be very happy," he replied and tears welled in his eyes. "I'm really not up to going, though, I'm sorry. But my best wishes go with you. Come back and see me later before I leave for the airport, please," and he reached out to them.

They took his hand for a moment. "Okay, kids, Chaplain Franklin is waiting. There will be a short reception in the dining hall afterwards. Maybe you'll feel like coming for punch and cake," Shirley said.

"Yeah, maybe so, I'll try," Curt responded.

The small chapel was lightly decorated with flowers remaining from the weekend, and the chaplain's assistant played soft organ music until all was ready. Shirley assisted Jan in her last-minute preparations. Adjusting the headpiece for her, she suddenly hugged her close. "That's for your mama. You are a beautiful bride. Now don't start bawling. Be happy, you're getting a darned good Joe for a husband. I've seen big love for you in his eyes since day one," she said.

A staff doctor served as best man and escorted Jan down the aisle while the organist played the wedding march. The ceremony was short but impressive, and each of the twelve attendees came up and offered their congratulations and best wishes while photographers snapped away.

Shortly after the reception began, Curt was rolled to the dining hall and toasted the newlyweds with punch. As the others gradually left the area, the survivors sat at a table for a farewell. "Folks, I want you to use my home here in Honolulu beginning today. I've called the housekeeper to pick you up. Then take the car and use it as your own," he said.

"Aah, Curt, we can't do that. We'll go to a hotel and stay until we can find a place, but it is very thoughtful and nice of you to offer these things to us," Bruce replied.

"Yes, it certainly is, and we appreciate you thinking of us like that," Jan added.

"Listen, I'm leaving in a little while, and I don't know how long I'll be gone. I really need someone there to look after the house for me. You'd be doing me a huge favor. I hope you will consider it."

"Well, if it's of some help to you, of course we'll go there and stay until you return. But on a rental basis! Meantime, we can look around a little slower and get an apartment close to the airport and all of that rot," Bruce ventured.

"Oh yeah, it will help me, but forget the rent stuff. I'll be more comfortable knowing you're there looking after things for me. By the way, my ex called this morning and told me she's kept up with our adventures since the news broke. She wants us to start over," Curt laughed softly, "and said she likes me better than anyone else she's encountered since we broke up."

"Are you going to try again?" Jan asked.

"I think so. She's coming to California to see me and we'll decide for sure. I've thought about it a lot since her call, and the more I think about it, the better I like it."

"Hey, that's great, man. I'm pleased for you," Bruce said.

"Mr. Myrick, it's time to leave for the airport. Are you ready, sir?" Sergeant Shwallon said as he entered the dining room.

"Yeah, all set. Well, folks, this is it. Be happy. I'll get in touch with you later. Bye," he said and waved as the medic pushed his wheelchair from the room.

Chapter Seventeen

Shirley came into the dining room just after Curt left. "Jan, Bruce, there's a lady in my office asking for you," she said and gestured over her shoulder with a thumb.

They walked with her toward the office. "Shirley, I don't know how we'll ever be able to thank you properly for all you did for us, but somehow, someday, we will," Jan said.

"You've already thanked me by what you did for *us*. Mainly I was just doing my job, and besides, I've enjoyed every minute of it. You two are special to me, and after the honeymoon is over, I want to talk with you, Jan, about what went on out there on that island," she replied and made motions with her eyes.

Jan giggled and Bruce's cheeks turned pink. "There's nothing to tell except what we wrote in those inventories, honestly," he said.

Shirley reached over and placed the back of her hand on his cheek, smiled and said, "Hmmm."

"Mr. and Mrs. Ryan," a small Japanese woman began, "I am Kumiko Hiroshige. Mr. Myrick has sent me to bring you to his house. The car is parked just outside. Come with me, please."

"We're pleased to meet you," Jan said.

Kumiko led them outside to a light blue Olds 88 and held the rear door open until they were seated. She went around to the front door and opened it, then gestured toward the hospital door. Shirley was there waving goodbye to them, and they returned the gesture. Kumiko drove past International Airport heading east toward Waikiki Beach. At the top of a small hill she turned into the drive of a medium-sized house constructed from hewn logs with a wood shingle roof and a porch of lava rocks. There was a garage attached and its door opened at the touch of a button. She drove in and stopped.

The house was decorated inside with immaculate wood carvings and the furniture was light teak. Modern appliances filled the kitchen and each of the three bedrooms held a four poster bed with a satin canopy. Both bathrooms had sunken tubs and shower stalls. A den off the living room had overstuffed furniture and one of the newer console radio-record players. As Jan and Bruce looked through the house, the doorbell rang and Kumiko hurried to answer. Then she summoned Bruce and Jan back into the living room.

"Mr. and Mrs. Ryan, I am Bob Wanafuchi," the stocky Japanese man said. "I am from Bishop Realty Company. Aloha."

Bruce shook his hand and Jan said it was a pleasure to meet him.

"I have papers that you need to sign for ownership of your home. Shall we do this now, or do you wish to wait for some reason. I know this is very short notice," he said.

"I don't understand what you mean by ownership, Mr. Wanafuchi, we don't own this house. Our friend, Curtis Myrick, asked us to come here and live temporarily while he is away," Bruce said.

Bob smiled, shook his head and reached into his briefcase to draw out a sheaf of papers. "Mr. Myrick is a fine gentleman, but he does not always tell his friends the whole truth. Especially about those things in their favor. He called this morning and told me to transfer ownership of this property and house to you. You see, he owns half-interest in Bishop Realty. It is yours already, but you must sign these papers so it can be recorded legally. We have taxes here, too," Wanafuchi said and laughed softly.

"Why, he can't give us his house just like that," Jan said.

"Oh, no, he *sold* it to you, and after you sign, I must collect the entire sum of money from you," he said and smiled.

"I don't know about this, Mr. Wanafuchi. I see what you're saying, but we didn't agree to buy the house," Bruce said,

Bob smiled again. "Mr. Ryan, this is a price you cannot refuse. One dollar and other considerations."

"Jan, what do you think?" Bruce asked.

"Gosh, I don't know. I've never experienced anything like this."

"Please, sir, madam, you must sign now. The transaction is already done. Whatever your doubts, the insurance is only in force if you have signed in case something should happen."

"Well, okay, we'll sign and take this up with Curt, I mean Mr. Myrick, later," Bruce said.

They signed the forms, paid a dollar and sat back staring at Wanafuchi in disbelief about what had just transpired.

"Thank you very much. Oh, I almost forgot. Here is the bill of sale for the automobile, and I will need another dollar for it," he said and extended a paper to Bruce.

Bruce gave him a dollar and accepted the form. "Thank you, and my congratulations. May your lives be happy and very fruitful ones together. Good day," Wanafuchi said and left hurriedly.

Kumiko rejoined Jan and Bruce after Bob left. "Mrs. Ryan, there is something that I need to discuss with you. Is it convenient to do that now?" she asked.

Jan looked at Bruce, then to her. "Yes, please do."

"I have been Mr. Myrick's housekeeper, as you know, and I come here each Wednesday to do my work. Do you wish me here on that day, or would you prefer another time?"

"Well, I don't know. This is all new to me. I haven't thought about a home and certainly not someone to work for me."

"I understand your feelings, and I am sorry about the confusion. You see, Mr. Myrick told me to come here every week for one year to work, and if the same day was not satisfactory with you to please change it to your wishes. He will pay me the same as before. My husband, Ito, is the gardener, and he comes each Friday. Is that satisfactory with you both?"

Bruce laughed and shook his head, then threw up his hands. "Yeah, Mrs. Hiroshige, those days will be fine. We don't mean to confuse you or anything of that nature, but as you said, there is confusion here already. We had no idea anything like this would happen."

She laughed softly. "Yes, I understand. Mr. Myrick told me this morning he planned to do these things and neither of you knew about them."

"It was to be a surprise wedding gift because you did so much for him and were so kind to him out there on the island."

"A surprise it certainly is. But I can't think of anything we did to warrant such a gift as this. We just all shared to survive and get off the island as soon so we could," Bruce said.

"Those are my sentiments too," Jan added.

"Mr. Myrick is a very nice and generous man. Ito and I have worked for him the past three years. Each Christmas he has given us an extra month's pay. He said others had been generous with him and he just wanted to share it with someone. He is a wealthy man here in the islands and is highly respected by all who know him. I have gone through the furniture to remove and pack all of his personal things. They are stored in the garage, and he will make arrangements to get them soon. Here are the keys to your house and car. I will leave now and return tomorrow as it is Wednesday. Thank you very much for your kindness to me, and may I, too, offer my congratulations and best wishes."

"Thank *you* for your kindness to *us*. I will have a thousand questions to ask you tomorrow," Jan said.

Kumiko smiled, "Very well, I will try to have a thousand answers for you by then. Goodbye until tomorrow."

After she left Jan said, "Ryan, can you beat this? I really can't believe it has happened to us. Married less than one day and we're home and auto owners in Hawaii with a maid and gardener, all paid for by someone we hardly know."

"No, I can't say that I can beat it, but there's something I want to show you out front, come on."

They went to the porch and Jan looked around questioningly. "Have you seen it yet?" he asked.

"It looks like a porch and lawn to me."

"Well, how about what the banisters are made of?"

"Oh, my goodness, it's lava! I guess we just can't get away from that on any island, huh?"

"Nope, and I wonder if Curt has thought about that?"

"Probably not," she said and turned to reenter the house.

"Oh, wait, there's one more thing," Bruce said and stretched his arms out to pick her up. "I have to carry you over the threshold, you know. That's required, I think."

Jan giggled as he made his way inside. He dropped her feet on
the floor and slipped his arms around her. "Okay, Mrs. Ryan, we
start right now making up for lost time."

Her hands glided over his shoulders and she smiled while
looking deeply into his eyes. Then her arms moved around his
neck as their lips met. After several lingering kisses she pulled free.
"Mr. Ryan, we started and have from now on to catch up. I want
to look this place over now. Then we have to think about what our
first married meal is going to be. The crab, breadfruit, and bamboo
shoots are all gone," she said and laughed.

Bruce had detected her tension as the last kiss continued.
"Okay, honey. Let's look the joint over, then we'll get in our Rocket
88 and go wherever they serve something other than crab, fish,
and breadfruit. How does a thick steak sound to you?"

"Like something straight out of heaven, especially if they have
French fries and beer to go with it, since I've lost six pounds. Hey,
I know just the place," she said.

He nodded and smiled. "Jan, things have moved very fast and
we've both been in a hectic situation, especially during the last
four days. If I'm coming on too strong, forgive me. You're the
beautiful woman that I love very much, and I'm afraid my
adrenaline might be pumping a little too heavily. Loosen up, we'll
let things progress at your pace for as long as you like."

She hugged him tightly and pecked his cheek. "Ryan, you're
very sweet. After dinner I'm getting into my personal spa with lots
of bubbles for a long bath, then we'll see if that four poster really
flies," she said as she pushed him toward the garage. "Let's go, I
don't think I like that grin on your face."

They lingered over the meal for a very long time discussing
whether to go on a honeymoon, and finally decided they were
already on one in a paradise other couples only dreamed about.
Darkness had fallen when they reached home. "I think that steak
was close to being out of this world, so I guess that makes it
heavenly," Jan said.

"It's definitely the best one I've had in a while. Have you been
to that restaurant often?" he asked.

"No, just a few times on layovers, but they're consistent. I've
never had a bad meal there before," she replied.

Bruce chuckled as they entered the house from the garage. "The brew wasn't half bad either, and I didn't realize how much I'd missed having ketchup with my meals," he said.

"Ryan, you and your coffee, now it's ketchup, too. Okay, tub, here I come," she said and giggled.

"While you do that, I'm going to call my parents with an announcement. Do you want to call yours too, or wait?" he said.

"Gosh, I forgot about that. I don't call them often enough I know, but, yes, I'll do it after my bath. What time is it in Houston now?"

"There's a four hour difference, so it's ten-thirty. That's not too late for me, my folks are night owls."

"Okay, I'll call by eleven or so."

Bruce dialed the operator and placed his call. Shortly Carolyn answered. "Hello, Mom. How are you, dad, and the kids?"

"We're all fine. It's good that you called, I've been waiting with blood in my eye. What took you so long?" she asked.

"So long, what do you mean?"

"Don't play coy with me boy, they reported your wedding on television earlier this evening and showed a picture of you and your wife."

"I can't believe it was on already."

"Oh, yes! Every time any of you three breathe they put it first on the news, and here I have to find out by the newscast that my first-born got married. What do you have to say for yourself?" she said and began giggling before he could answer.

"I knew you were picking at me, but it's hard to get the real voice tones on these cracking lines."

"Well, I know now what ailed you in some of those earlier pictures. You were moping around lovesick over that woman. I can always tell, so next time don't deny it."

"How can you always tell?"

"Mamas just can. I told your dad if you let that beautiful girl get away, he would have to come out there and bash your head in to get you out of your misery."

Bruce laughed. "Yeah, you're probably right. Beautiful she is and a fine woman, too. I'll write soon and tell you all about her."

"I already know about her."

"Huh? How do you already know?"

"Well, when the news came on, I called her mother and she was watching, too. You know we talked before when you were first rescued, and now we've told all about both of you. Her family is meeting us tomorrow for dinner, and we'll drag out all of the skeletons from both closets. How about that?"

"Whatever's fair for both," he said and they laughed.

"Son, your dad and I congratulate you. I know Janice will make you a fine wife. Be good to her and give us a grandchild real soon."

"Well, that's a roger on the first, but you know we've been married less than twelve hours. That second will take a little time."

"Don't go smarting off to me, boy, do like I say!" she snapped and they laughed for a moment. Thanks for calling, son. Take care of Janice and yourself. We love you."

"Love you too, bye."

He hung up the telephone and lingered at the small table in reflection for a long moment.

Jan called from the bath. "Did your call get through okay?"

"Yeah, and would you believe they reported our wedding on television in Houston this evening?"

"You don't mean it!"

"Yep, my mom knew it and so does yours. She was watching the same newscast, and they have already spoken with each other again to discuss the latest—us!"

"Well, I'd better get out of the tub and call, too. I expect my name is mud already, since I was supposed to be on my way home and practically there by this time."

"Yeah, that's a good idea. Mama gave me down the country about not calling sooner."

"Did she *really*?"

"Nah, she was only kidding. She gave us congrats and good wishes. Oh! She also said to get them a grandchild soon."

Jan giggled. "They aren't in much of a hurry, are they?"

"No, not much."

She came from the bathroom wearing light yellow pajamas, and Bruce pursed his lips, then moved his head from side to side. "What's wrong? I know you've seen girls in pj's before, like at the movies."

"Honey, ain't nothing wrong, and yeah, I've seen 'em before, but not this one with 'em whut fits like peeling on an apple."

"Ooh, a dirty old man. I'd better get my call going. It's getting late in Texas."

Bruce got a bath while Jan called, and after he was dressed for bed, she had finished.

"Well, how did your announcement go over, like a lead balloon?"

"No, everything went just fine. Mom cried a little when I told her Shirley hugged me for her at the wedding. She enjoyed talking with your mother, and they plan to meet tomorrow for dinner. As you say, I guess they'll give us a going over," she said and they laughed.

"Well, that's okay by us, huh? They don't really know everything like they claim. Mom said I had been looking mopey on television because I was lovesick over you."

"Hmmm, and were you?"

"Yeah, I reckon so," he said and chuckled.

"That's interesting. Maybe I should have gone on to Houston, had a talk with her, then come back here."

"Nah, that wouldn't have worked out. I might even have flown away with a blonde by then."

"Oh! Well, then I'll keep that in mind."

He laughed. "But you didn't, I didn't, and if I'm lovesick, then I need treatment, right?"

"Let's see. I've had dinner, a bath and made my call. Seems like there was another little something, but I don't remember what it was. Maybe it will come back to me in a few days," she said and Bruce stood looking at her, grinning.

She went to him, smiled, then embraced him ardently while nudging him toward the four poster.

Chapter Eighteen

Day Forty-one

Bruce reported for work in the early morning and spent the remainder of the morning doing paperwork, then he began operations orientation.

Jan called Am-Mex to tender her resignation with the airline, but representatives asked her to consider a part-time job in their local office instead. She agreed to think it over. Then she went through their new home making an inventory of what they needed to set up housekeeping. During the afternoon Kumiko told her that she had only asked five hundred questions, and she could ask the other five hundred next Wednesday.

At day's end, the newlyweds assessed their first full day and decided that, overall, it had been good for them both. "Ryan, the company asked me to consider working two days each week in sales and public relations rather than accept my resignation. What do you think?" Jan asked.

"I think you should do whatever you want to. After all, you're the one that'll have to rise and shine."

"Yeah, that's one of the things I thought about first. But two days shouldn't be all that bad, I'll try it for a while."

"Sounds good to me. You can always stop if the rising or shining becomes a problem."

Day Fifty-one

"Would you like to have some Texas-style barbecue?" Bruce asked Jan in the late evening.

"Oh, yes, I was thinking of that just the other day. Can you do the real thing?"

"Nah, and never could. But there's a guy on my crew from Fort Worth who says he can cook it better than my mama."

"Well, invite him and his wife over, right away!"

Bruce laughed. "He's not married. He's a redheaded, green-eyed Irishman. He said he was born under a TKO and has been knocked out with women ever since."

"Ryan, what are you talking about?"

"His name is Thomas Kerry O'Hara, you know, TKO," he replied and laughed.

"Aah, be serious. I want some barbecue!"

"Okay. I'm getting to that. Tom is about the most bashful fellow I've ever encountered. He's a wreck with girls, but a darned good controller. I figure if we invite Shirley to come out, she'll be good for him, you know, someone to take charge and lead the way."

"She might not want to lead the way. Most girls want the boy to lead them."

"Yeah, but I thought to ask her. I told Tom a little about her and he wants to meet her *bad*. They're about the same age, thirty, I'd guess. That's a little high for a fellow trying to get a girl, most are already married by that age."

"Hmmm, you might be right. I'll call her Monday and see what she thinks about it. He's not, well, you know, ugly is he?"

"No, he's an average looking fellow, tall and I mean really bashful. When our forty-year-old secretary talks to him it brings on something close to spasms. I think she kind of enjoys that, just kidding around to see him squirm."

"I've had misgivings about being a matchmaker before. It's just never been my thing," she said.

"Mine either, but I like Tom and Shirley, so I'll make an exception in this case. Mainly, I'd like to invite her out because of all she did for us. They can work out the developments themselves."

Day Fifty-three

"Major Marshall," a pleasant voice responded after the telephone rang several times.

"Hi, Shirley, this is Jan Adams, I mean Ryan. How are you?"

"Hi, I'm fine. I don't know whether married life is agreeing with you are not. You don't even know your name. Maybe it's because you're so elated," she replied and laughed.

Jan laughed too. "It would have to be the latter, no complaints at all. I've been looking for this good ol' boy since high school. He's a real gem," Jan responded.

"Well, that's great. I knew you two were meant for each other. What can we do for you, Mrs. Ryan?"

"Bruce and I are having a Texas-style barbecue this Wednesday evening, and we'd like to know if you'll come to our home and join us?"

"Yes, I can. What's the occasion?"

"There's a guy on Bruce's crew from Fort Worth who claims to be the best barbecue man west of the Mississippi. I'm starving for good barbecue. It has been months, and besides, this fellow wants to meet you."

"Oh? How does he know me?"

"Boys talk too," she said and giggled.

"Tell me something about him. But, I'm coming for the barbecue no matter what you say about the guy."

"He's thirty, tall, average looking with bright red hair and green eyes. A full-blooded Irishman and has the worst case of the bashfuls west of the River."

"A bashful Irishman? This I have to see. I'll be there, what time should I show?"

"Anytime, five, I guess."

Bruce was off duty Wednesday, and Ito came to help him construct a small pit for barbecuing. Tom arrived in early afternoon and began cooking. Jan initiated small talk with him and quickly saw that he was indeed bashful which was more pronounced by his blushing easily and often. But she also sensed that his sincerity and moral fiber were above reproach. Shirley came at five-thirty and the meal began shortly. Afterwards, they sipped beer and made small talk until eight, mostly about their good fortune, courtesy of Curtis Myrick. "Jan, please show me to the powder room," Shirley said and they went inside.

After a few moments Shirley began, "Tom is a nice guy, and I'm glad that you introduced us. You're right, a bashful Irishman, and I didn't know they made any of those. He's cute and witty and he asked me for a date Saturday."

"Did you accept?"

"Yes. He doesn't talk much, but what there is counts. We have a lot in common, surprisingly. He even has relatives living in Louisville, Kentucky. We're going sightseeing, then to a movie. I've never been to several of the well-known attractions here in Honolulu, and he wants me to go and see them."

"I'm glad you two hit it off so well. He's a great cook, and we'll try our best to get him back again *soon*! Of course, you're always welcome here, and I'm giving you a standing invitation for whenever you want to come over," Jan said.

"That's very nice, and I'll take you up on it often. Both the fellowship and barbecue in this house were outstanding."

Shirley and Tom left shortly with a promise to return soon.

Day Sixty

The telephone rang in the early evening. When Jan answered a well-modulated, woman's voice said, "Jan?"

"Yes."

"This is Ingrid Heilbron, Curtis Myrick's former wife. May I call you Jan? I've heard so much about you and Bruce, it's as though I know you both well."

"Oh, please do, and how is Curt?"

"He's much better, thank you, and progressing wonderfully. They did surgery two weeks ago and started him on a physical therapy program to regain motion on his left side. He can move both limbs some and the numbness is in slow remission. The doctor told me this morning his prognosis is very good for recovery, up to a point—about eighty or ninety percent of what it was previously."

"That is great! Bruce and I both wish him the very best for a speedy recovery. Please tell him."

"Oh, I shall. He speaks of you two every day and tells me how nice and thoughtful you were to him on the island. If there is anyone on earth that he thinks more of or cares for, I've never heard their name."

"We think a great deal of Curt, too! You know, he was primarily responsible for our getting off that island. He came up with the idea of using salvage from the bomber, then told us how to assemble the material to make the radio work. We won't forget him for that, nor for this beautiful house he gave us. It's still hard to believe anyone would just up and hand someone their home and automobile free and clear of all debt."

Ingrid laughed softly. "Rick, Curt, spoke with Kumiko the day after you moved in, and she told him quite a story. I've never seen him so happy about anything before or since."

"Kumiko is so nice to us. That's another gift. She said Curt told her to come here every week for the next year, along with her husband, to keep our place up. We can't get over that either, and want to compensate Curt for the property for the rest of our lives."

"He wouldn't think of accepting anything from you for that house. What he did was give you a well-deserved gift. Enjoy it and be happy. Rick is very pleased that he could do those things for you."

"All we can say then is a simple 'thank you,' and that doesn't seem to cover the situation completely nor accurately."

"Believe me, coming from you and Bruce, that's enough."

"Well, tell him he's a friend above and beyond all friends."

"Oh, I shall."

"Do you suppose he will come back here after finishing the treatment program?" Jan asked.

"We really haven't discussed things that far ahead yet, but he did say wherever I want to live, he's for that, too," Ingrid replied.

"Are you getting married again?"

Ingrid giggled. "Well, I proposed and he accepted."

"Did you really?"

"Yes, sort of. I spoke with him before he left Hawaii and told him that I liked him better than anyone else I'd met since we split during the war. He told me the feeling was mutual."

"That's nice. I'm happy for the both of you."

"Thank you. I think we were just young before and probably didn't know how to deal with the tension and stresses of the war plus our own personal feelings and anxieties."

"Well, it certainly was an unsettling period for millions of people. I'm not surprised that it got to the two of you.

"So, how are you and Bruce fairing?"

"We're getting along beautifully. He's one heck of a man, and I love him more each day."

"From what Rick has said, that's very understandable. And what are you doing to occupy yourself?"

"I've gone back to the airline for two days each week, not flying, however. I'm in sales and public relations this time."

"That's nice, you will probably enjoy it."

"Yeah, it's not as hectic as the flying game."

"Jan, I just called to see how you and Bruce were coping. Rick was concerned that perhaps the house had put stress on you or something."

"No, not at all, and we thought of trying to contact him to see how he was progressing. But we've both been so busy getting settled and all, we just haven't taken the time to get back to the doctor here and trace Curt through him."

"Of course. I'll bring him up to date on the both of you. Please say hello to Bruce for Rick. You have his best wishes and regards, and mine!" she said and then gave a telephone number where she or Curt could be reached.

They said goodbye then, and when Bruce came home from work, Jan gave him Ingrid's message.

"Well, I'm happy for Curt. He's a good guy. I hope that he and Ingrid will remarry and live happily ever after," he said and chuckled.

"Yes, so do I. She sounded very nice."

"Adams, I've wondered, what if I hadn't proposed to you when I did. Where would we be now?"

"Ryan, I would have gone to Houston to see my parents, lollygagged around for a while and then come back here. You were not getting away, I'd already decided that."

He laughed and reached across the bed to squeeze her hand.

"Now, I have a question for you. What if I had said no?"

"Ugh! Somebody would have picked out one of them pine boxes for me and sung sad, sad music," he said, grinning, and left to smoke a cigarette.

Jan laughed, fluffed the pillow, and turned off the lamp on her side of the bed.

Bruce returned shortly, clicked off his lamp, lay back and sighed heavily. "Woman, you know what?"

"No, man, what?"

"You are prettier every time I see you."

"Uh oh! Even the ugliest natives are beginning to look good to the troops. Isn't that what you said?"

"Nah, I said you ain't no native and you sure ain't ugly," he replied and moved over to her.

"Well, thank you, sir, I think."

Hawaii is also beautiful in total darkness.

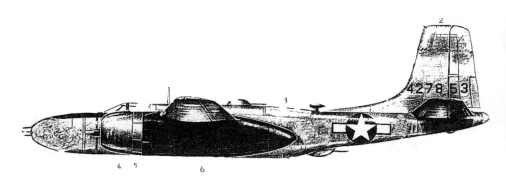

Douglas A-26 "Invader"

1. Radio antenna and aerial wire
2. Vertical stabilizer
3. Gunner's compartment
4. Engine cowling
5. Cowl flaps
6. Landing gear doors

Douglas B-26 "Invader" or the USAAF A-26
USAAF photo

Republic P-47 "Thunderbolt"
USAAF photo

Lockheed 1049 (or the military C-121) Constellation or "Connie"
Photo courtesy of U.S. Army Aviation Museum, Ft. Rucker, AL

North American P-51 "Mustang" (later redesignated F-51 by the USAF)
USAAF photo

Douglas DC-6 "Loadmaster"
Photo courtesy of McDonnell Douglas Aircraft Company

Boeing B-29 "Superfortress"
USAAF photo

Douglas DC-4 or military C-54
Photo courtesy of McDonnell Douglas Aircraft Company

Grumman SA-16 "Albatross"
Photo courtesy of USAF Museum, Dayton, OH